Shard

of the

Sun

OTHER BOOKS

Dragon Riders of Osnen

Trial by Sorcery
A Bond of Flame
The Warrior's Call
The Coin of Souls
Wing of Terror
Eyes of Stone
Tooth and Claw
The Servant of Souls
Smoke and Shadow
The Dark Rider

Marked by the Dragon

Scale of the Dragon
Egg of the Dragon
Call of the Dragon
Wrath of the Dragon

The Fallen King Chronicles

Dragonsphere
The Fallen King
The Valiant King
The Restored King

Dragons of Isentol

Throne of Deceit
Rune Marked
Empire of Serpents

Shard

of the

Sun

RICHARD FIERCE

Dragonfire Press

e-Book ISBN: 978-1-947329-16-4

Print ISBN: 978-1-958354-05-6

Second Edition: 2022

For Cindy Lingerfelt,

who asked me to finally write this one.

Introduction

I have climbed the peaks of Hell, mountains formed from the souls of sin. I have bathed in the fires of brimstone, flames fueled by souls consumed with hatred. I have talked with demons, their lips sweet with the promises of power ...

Hell loomed before him.

Ferrin cursed his weak body. Time had taken its toll on his shell of flesh, and he knew all too well what he was destined for. There had to be a way to escape his fate. And the answer, he believed, lay within the vexatious city of Ravendale. Those blasted warrior-priests protected it. While he and his apprentices could easily crush them, they could not get past the magical shield they had erected over the city. Ferrin had tried once, much to his dismay, to enter the city by force. He lost several apprentices and the shield had burned him severely.

The many scars covering his body were a testament to the power of the shield. He gripped the worn wood of his staff, putting most of his weight on it, and shuffled feebly over to the window. One of his novices, Vius, stood by his door at all times in the event he needed something.

The young man moved as if to help him, but the piercing look he gave the apprentice stopped the man cold. "I am not helpless!" Ferrin said angrily. Once, he would have killed over an indiscretion like that. But now ... those seeking to learn the darker side of magic were few. He needed them all, much to his dislike. It was another reminder of his weakness. He pushed the window open and was assaulted by a blast of icy wind. The gust blew his hood back, whipping it around wildly.

The cold wasteland of Eurn was a cruel and harsh land. The days were cold and merciless, the nights much more severe. But it served his purposes. Out of the prying eyes of those who sought his destruction, Ferrin was free to do as he wished in secret. The sky was black. No stars could be seen through the mass of dark clouds that brought snow falling in copious amounts. Ferrin stared out at the empty land, barren and covered in winter's breath.

It had been eighty years. Eighty long years since his escape from Hell. He admitted his foolishness to himself. Attempting to take over the nightmarish land of demons, he found that he was sorely overpowered. He knew the truth of life in the moment of his escape. And it drove him to find a way to avoid going back.

His magic could no longer prolong the inevitable. His body was beginning to fail. The knowledge of possessing another body through the power of his will had been lost during the war with the demons. Ferrin needed something strong enough to rejuvenate his body. The priests of Ravendale were always preaching about eternal life. Yet Ferrin believed there was more to their claims than just metaphorical theologies.

Their savior was, after all, his own nephew. And the faith that had blossomed after the war only added to his frustration. Ferrin himself had once been a priest of the gods, and he had willingly chosen the other side. But these people believed something different.

"No matter," he whispered to himself. As he stared up into the sky, he heard a loud rumbling like thunder followed by a bright flash. Ferrin leaned forward, sticking his head out into the whipping wind. Snow and ice pelted his face, but he kept his focus on the sky. Through gaps in the clouds he could see a streaking light steadily descending toward the earth. *Could it be?*

"You!" he cried. He heard Vius approach. Ferrin pulled his head back inside and turned his eyes on the young man. "Get the others, quickly. I have a task for you."

Chapter 1

Broderick threw some herbs into the pot over the fire and stirred it with a small spoon. The night air was warm. The light of the moon reflected off the clear waters of the Paddleford Lake. His home was built on the edge of it. The lake was in the center of the woods at the base of a large mountain. There weren't many people that lived near the lake. The house had been in Broderick's family for as long as anyone could remember and was passed down through the generations.

Broderick's parents had died of disease several years earlier. He was almost twenty-three, with short blonde hair and large, bright green eyes. He was a few inches short of six feet, with broad shoulders and strong, corded muscles. He earned a living cutting down trees and selling the wood.

He leaned in close to the pot and smelled the soup. It made his mouth water. He hadn't eaten since noon and he was starving. He grabbed a cloth and pulled the pot off the fire. He quickly poured its contents into a wooden bowl before he burned his hand. A loud explosion that sounded like thunder startled him. A flash of light in the sky caught his attention and Broderick watched as it streaked across the heavens. His eyes widened in shock as he realized the streaking light was coming in his direction.

Before he could make up his mind as to what direction he should run, the light came roaring over his house and splashed into the lake. A wave of heat washed over him and he cringed back. The water sizzled and bubbled where the object had hit. A strange light shone from the water, which made Broderick curious. "Might be a fallen star," he said excitedly to himself. He could sell it for a high price in the market. His parents had found one when he was a boy and made a small fortune.

The more he thought about it, the more excited he got. He quickly stripped down to his loincloth and waded out into the water. The lake was roughly twenty feet at its deepest spot. When Broderick reached the point where he had to stand on the tip of his toes, he breathed in deep and dove down into the water. With the moon shining unhindered, Broderick could easily see through the clear water.

He spotted where the light was shining and went up for air. After another deep breath, he swam down to the lake floor and began to swim closer. As he neared what he assumed was a meteorite, the water became noticeably warmer. The light was beginning to dim, so he swam faster. He didn't want to lose sight of it.

Broderick reached the spot and could feel the pressure in his lungs building. He needed to breath, but he didn't want to risk losing the rock. He grabbed at the fading light and a searing pain shot through his flesh. He tried to cry out but got a mouthful of water instead. He clutched the stone tightly and began to choke. He panicked and pushed off the floor of the lake to try to reach the surface. The burning in his lungs intensified as he sucked in more water.

The thought occurred to him that he was probably going to die. In the middle of the lake out in the wilderness where no one would even know he was gone. No one to mourn his passing.

As he broke the surface of the water, he began sputtering water out and trying to gasp in air. He could no longer feel the stone in his hand; the flesh was numb. Somehow he managed to navigate to the shore. He crawled on his hands and knees to the cooking fire before he lost consciousness.

—

Broderick awoke to the sound of birds chirping. He was laying face down and his head felt like it was going to explode. He grunted as he pushed himself up off the ground and stood on shaky legs. It was morning. The woods were alive with the sounds of animals and a light breeze had the trees swaying. His fire had died some time during the night. His bowl was where he left it, the soup long since cold.

He looked around dazedly. Then he remembered. The shooting star, his swim and subsequent almost drowning incident. Where was that rock, anyway? He saw it next to the ring of rocks that surrounded his cooking fire. He retrieved it and held it up in the air. It wasn't a rock. At least, not one he'd ever seen before. It was clear like a crystal, flat, and smooth. It was small and easily fit in the palm of his hand.

That's when he noticed his hand. The skin was completely gone. The muscle lay bare and unprotected. Here and there it looked like bone was showing. Surprisingly he felt no pain. He could move his fingers and even grabbed a stick to see if it hurt to use the hand. Nothing. It was as if the skin wasn't even missing.

After starting another fire and warming his soup, he ate and went about his normal morning routine. He had almost filled his wagon with enough wood to sell at the market the day before. He had one more tree to cut and then he could travel to Myrwood to sell the lumber. He grabbed his ax and went to work, cutting along the measured lines he had made yesterday. His hand still did not bother him. As the day went by, he didn't even bother to check his hand. Noon came and went by the time he finished his task. He was walking toward the lake to wash up when he saw something fall from a nearby tree.

He walked over and saw a baby bird lying dead on the ground. "Poor little thing," he muttered to himself. He knelt down and picked up the lifeless creature with his disfigured hand and dug a small hole with his other. He was about to place the dead bird into the hole when he felt it move. He watched in amazement as the baby bird stood up in his hand. "You weren't dead after all," he said. "Just a little stunned. Let's get you back in your nest." He looked up into the tree to see how high the nest was. Unfortunately it was just out of his reach.

He gently placed the bird in a leather pouch on his waist and climbed the tree. He reached the branch with the nest and placed the bird back in it. "No more suicide attempts," he told the bird. Then he climbed back down. He went inside his house to get a towel and some fresh clothes. He would need to be at least somewhat presentable if he was going to do business in Myrwood. As he was going through his clothes trying to decide what to wear, he noticed a large shadow pass by his window. He glanced out the window but didn't see anything.

He was about to go back digging through his clothes when he saw another shadow pass by. And another. And another. He walked over to the window and his eyes widened in terror. An oversized hand smashed through the window and tried to grab him.

Broderick barely leapt back in time to avoid being crushed. The hand disappeared and then he saw several large forms that resembled men standing outside his home. "*Giants*!" he breathed in amazement. His parents had often told him tales of giants who lived on the mountain. As a child, the tales were exciting. As he grew older, he doubted the truth of them and eventually stopped humoring his parents.

Yet here were a few of them. They were each carrying what appeared to be a club, though to Broderick they seemed more like small trees. One of them brought his club forward into the wall and it crashed in on itself. Broderick cursed and ran out of his house, narrowly avoiding a club that came bashing down through the ceiling. He grabbed his ax off the porch as he leapt down the stairs. Those creatures were tearing up his house for reasons he couldn't begin to fathom.

Broderick turned to look back and saw the giants were coming his direction. They were slow, lumbering creatures, but with their elongated legs they traveled long distances. He guessed they were all at least twelve feet in height except one. He was slightly taller than the others and wore a cape made from the fur of the mountain lions that inhabited the region. Broderick had no idea what to do. He certainly couldn't outrun them. He would tire long before he reached any civilized lands that could defend against them. He looked to the wagon. His horses were attached and ready for travel. He wouldn't be able to free them before the giants killed him.

The taller one said something that Broderick didn't understand. His voice was like the rumbling of boulders that occasionally tumbled down the mountain. They all ceased walking and just stared at him. If he were going to run, now was the time. He turned and fled. He got several yards before he risked glancing back at them. They were all still standing still. Just as he was turning his gaze back around, he saw that one of the giants started after him.

"Crap!" he growled. He ran faster, pumping his legs furiously. A loud screeching noise filled the air. It sounded like a bird, but he didn't have to time wonder at the sound. His mind raced with places he could try to hide. They all seemed stupid. The giant was quickly closing on him. His lungs and muscles were already starting to burn. He was breathing too heavily to keep his pace much longer. He heard a crash behind him and looked just in time to see the giant swinging its club in a wide arc. Broderick was lucky enough to avoid the bone crushing blow. The giant tried to stomp down on him but he changed direction and sprinted toward the lake.

Without thinking he leapt straight into the water. The water felt cool on his flesh. He dived under and swam as fast as his legs could kick. He felt the water surge around him as the giant followed him into the lake. Broderick came up for air and heard a ruckus where the other giants were but didn't bother to look. The giant that followed him raised its club to pound him.

Broderick sucked in his breath and dove under the water. The force of the giant's blow was lessened by the water, but when it struck him it still hurt like hell. It reminded him of the time a tree fell the wrong way and slammed into him. Had he been struck outside the water, there was no doubt in his mind that he would be dead. By some grace he was still alive. The air had been knocked from him and he struggled to get above the water. He broke the surface expecting to see the club bearing down on him. Instead, he saw the giant swatting at something around its face with its free hand.

Broderick painfully wiped the water from his eyes and was about to swim away when he spotted several birds swooping in to claw at the giant's face. The giant roared angrily in pain and kept trying to slap the pesky creatures away. Broderick glanced in the direction of the other giants and found them in the same situation. Birds of all species and sizes were swooping down and attacking the humanoid creatures. The giant in the water managed to hit a few out of the air, but more took their place. The sky seemed to come alive as at least a hundred birds took flight from the trees and joined in the battle.

Broderick noticed that where the giant was standing the water only came up to its ankles. In his panicked state, he had almost forgotten that he still had his ax. It seemed like a suicidal idea, but he decided to use the distraction of the birds to launch his own attack on the giant. He swam back toward the giant, easing slowly closer to make sure he didn't get stepped on. The thought of birds coming to his rescue seemed odd to him, but he didn't question his luck.

Broderick hefted his ax up and drew it back as he would chop at a tree. He was about to swing it when he noticed multiple puss filled sores on the giant's left ankle. Apparently the creature must have stepped in some toxic plants. He smirked as he struck a powerful blow to the giant's infected flesh. The ax cleaved right through the flesh, spilling puss and blood into the water. The giant's roar was louder up close. Birds swarmed around its face, scratching and pecking.

Broderick struck the giant's ankle again. Flesh and tendons separated from one another and the giant's leg crumpled under its weight. The giant fell backward into the lake, water splashing everywhere and waves rolling across the surface. Broderick tried to get out of the lake but the waves slammed into him, pushing him off his feet. They also pushed him onto the shore. He scrambled to his feet and turned to see the giant thrashing around in the water. The creature fell into the deeper area of the lake and couldn't seem to drag itself out of the water. The birds didn't help either. They kept diving in at its face.

He looked back toward the other giants. They were gone, leaving an obvious path of destruction in their flight from the birds. He made his way back to his house. With danger gone, his mind was free to wonder what had happened. He considered the tales of his parents and wondered how they knew about the giants. *Had they seen them before? If so, how had they survived?* Without the miraculous help of the birds, he would be dead right now.

As he approached his damaged house, he noticed the baby bird sitting at the edge of its nest. It appeared to be staring at him. There was something in the bird's eyes that unnerved him. Something … intelligent, knowing. *Did that bird call the others?*

"Of course it didn't," he said aloud. "It's just a bird." He didn't bother changing clothes but did bring them with him. He found his wagon some ways down the path. The giants had obviously spooked the horses and they fled. The weight of the wagon and the wood, however, kept them from going very far. He climbed onto the bench and took the leather reins in both hands, looping them under his pinkie finger and up through his fist before draping them over the thumbs of both hands. He gently flicked them and said, "Go."

The horses seemed to calm at his command and obeyed immediately, pulling the heavy wagon down the worn path. The horses were a gift from his cousin a year ago. His cousin had termed them 'Brabants'. Massive beasts, they stood a little over fifteen hands high. Their heads were relatively small when compared to their necks, which were thick and muscular. Their shoulders, quarters, and upper body were heftily built and spoke volumes about their strength.

Their legs were small but thick and only slightly feathered towards the bottom. If it weren't for the huge demand of lumber, he would never be able to afford them. They each ate over forty pounds of combined grain and hay and drank up to eighteen gallons of water *a day*. He was thankful to live on a lake. Thinking about the horses brought his cousin to mind. Broderick missed him. His cousin was a wealthy landowner and farmed honeysuckle.

Broderick looked back to ensure the giants had not returned. He didn't see or hear anything out of the ordinary. If the giant in the water didn't get itself out of the lake, it would be long dead by the time he got back from Myrwood. His cousin was in for quite a story, indeed. He leaned his back against the wagon and made himself comfortable. He reached into his leather pouch and pulled the rock out. In a few hours he would reach the city of Myrwood. In a few hours, he would be as rich as his cousin.

Chapter 2

Myrwood was a sprawling metropolitan. It bustled with commerce from sunrise to sunset, with vendors and artists coming from all over Rundäë to sell their wares. The city was old, built long before the invasion of demonic hordes that had nearly destroyed the human population. After the war, it was one of the first cities to be re-inhabited. Broderick could see the various dwellings, built of stone and wood, jutting up from the landscape. The city had been built in a deep valley surrounded by rolling green hills.

From his vantage point, he could see the twisting streets crowded with people. Several large warehouses were located outside of the city to hold inbound wagons until nightfall. The streets were normally so crowded that wagons were not able to enter the city until they cleared. Broderick knew this, of course, and so planned to visit one of the taverns after trying to sell his meteorite.

Farmland covered a lot of the hillsides. His cousin's lands were most notable. Acres upon acres were covered with honeysuckle. Rows of trellis so long that he could not see the end of them were used to grow the bright yellow flowered vines. The nectar of the honeysuckle was highly valued. Each flower only produced a few drops, and to produce enough for the kind of production his cousin was responsible for required a *lot* of land. Aside from the nectar (which was the major source of income), the vines had strongly fibrous stems and were used for binding and textiles. The flowers also produced an intense fragrance favored among the nobles.

As Broderick neared the city, he steered his wagon to one of the warehouses. A man in uniform approached, followed by a scribe. "Good afternoon, sir," the scribe greeted. "What goods will you be checking into the city?" Broderick returned the greeting with a smile. "I bring lumber." The scribe carried sheaves of paper and a piece of charcoal. He scribbled something down, muttering various numbers and names to himself. He looked up at Broderick, his face scrunching in thought. "Remind me again of your name?"

"Broderick," he told the scribe. The man's face lit up with recognition. "Ah! I knew it started with a 'B'. You know the protocol for wagon deliveries is to wait until nightfall, but fortunately for you we are short on lumber and need the delivery immediately." The scribe turned to the man in the uniform. "Pay the man, please. And then have them bring the wagon in through the eastern gate." The man nodded and tossed a small purse of gold coins to Broderick.

The scribe looked back to Broderick. "We will have one of our men bring the wagon in. And don't worry about your horses or wagon. Once the lumber is unloaded, they will bring the wagon back to this warehouse for your retrieval whenever you are ready to leave."

"Very well," Broderick replied. He rolled up the clean clothes he brought with him and made sure none of his leather pouches had come loose from his belt. Nodding to the scribe, he climbed down from the wagon and made his way to one of the many points of entry.

Guards checked everyone coming in to ensure the safety of the city. Weapons were not allowed inside, and neither were any goods. Everything had to be checked into the warehouses and brought in by the workers of Myrwood. Broderick entered the city quicker than most seeking entrance as he was not carrying anything in with him except clothing.

The bustle of the city was overwhelming to most people. The amount of foot traffic that traveled through the streets day to day was considerable. Hundreds of people crammed the streets, each trying to move through the crowd with an air of self importance. Broderick laughed at them. The majority of them were barely above poverty. He muscled his way through the crowds as well, navigating his way towards a shop known as the Mercantile. A middle aged man known as Torg owned it. His shop was a place where, if one had enough money, anything could be found.

Broderick pushed his way through the current of people and onto the street that housed the shop. It was less crowded than the main road but still congested. A bell jingled as he entered the shop and Torg greeted him. Torg had once been a soldier, with large muscles and a resume of deeds to be envied. The man Broderick looked at was a shell of that former glory. Torg had a huge belly and stooped forward. The center of his head was bald, while the rest of his hair had turned to a grayish white. His beard was the same color as the hair on his head, but much thicker. A long wooden counter separated Torg's goods and the customers who entered.

"Good to see you again, Torg," Broderick said. Torg smiled and extended his hands. "If it isn't my favorite customer," the shop owner replied. Broderick very much doubted that. He had only visited the Mercantile a handful of times. The truth was Torg said that to every customer. "What brings you into my world today?"

Broderick withdrew the rock from his pouch and laid it on the countertop. Torg picked it up and eyed it. "It's a meteorite," Broderick said. "It fell from the sky last night near my house. How much for it?" Broderick was expecting a huge payday.

Torg turned it over in his hands, eyeing every detail. "Nothing," he answered. Broderick's mouth dropped. "What do you mean nothing?"

Torg laid it back onto the counter. "It's an interesting piece, I'll give you that. But it is not a meteorite." Broderick raised an eyebrow. "It fell from the sky." Torg smiled disarmingly. "I'm not saying it didn't. I'm saying it isn't a meteorite." Broderick scratched his chin. "Then what it is?"

Torg shrugged. "I haven't the slightest idea, to be honest. But it is pretty. Let me see, I'll give you ..." he paused, looking at the smooth rock again, "twenty gold." Broderick snorted derisively. "No thanks." He grabbed the rock and started to leave. "Wait," he heard Torg say. Broderick stopped but didn't turn around. "Twenty-five gold, and your choice of anything in the shop."

Broderick shook his head. "I'd rather—" his words were drowned out by a scream from outside. Broderick stepped outside to see what was going on. A crowd had quickly formed around something. Broderick noticed his wagon and horses nearby. "What happened?" he asked someone walking away from the crowd. The man shook his head sadly. "Poor girl was run over by the horses," the man answered.

Broderick was crushed. A child run over by *his* horses. What else could go wrong? He pushed through the crowd to find a girl, no more than ten, lying on the ground in a pool of blood. "Oh no," he whispered voicelessly. It was Claire. His cousin's daughter. Tears flooded his eyes as he bent down beside her. "What happened?" he cried out.

Nobody answered. His dream of becoming rich was the last thing on his mind now. He gingerly pulled her into his arms and stroked her hair. He shook his head over and over. *This can't be happening.* He stared into her face and remembered when his cousin had given him the news that his wife was having a baby. It was believed his cousin's wife was barren for years, and then she got pregnant. Claire was a miracle child.

Broderick could faintly hear the sound of the city guard coming. Through watery eyes he thought he saw Claire's eyes flutter. He wiped the tears away so he could see clearly. Nothing. It was a trick of his mind, seeing what he wanted to see. And then he heard someone in the crowd gasp. He looked up to see several people wide eyed and pointing. "She moved!" someone yelled.

He looked back down to see Claire staring at him. "Claire! Are you all right? Where does it hurt?" The little girl didn't answer at first but just stared at him. Her eyes … there was something in her eyes that seemed familiar, but he couldn't place it. He hugged her tightly. "I'm not in pain," she finally answered. Broderick searched her for any wounds but found none. "Are you sure?" he asked. "You are covered in blood."

Claire nodded her head. "I'm fine. I remember the horses didn't stop. They hurt me and everything went dark. I couldn't see anything. And then I opened my eyes and you were here." She smiled. "I have missed you, Uncle Broderick!" She returned his hug.

Broderick could hear the familiar voice of his cousin shouting. "Claire! Claire, where are you?" The crowd parted to let the man through. Broderick looked up to see his cousin Derrick.

Derrick saw the blood on his daughter and went into a panic. "What happened? Is she injured? Call for my physicians!" Broderick shook his head. "She seems fine, cousin." As if to prove his words, Claire got up and ran to her father. "Really daddy, I am fine." Derrick hugged his daughter close. "I told you not to walk in the road," he scolded lovingly.

"I'm sorry, daddy. I won't do it again." Derrick nodded his head and looked at the man who had been driving the wagon. "You," he said menacingly, pointing. "Consider yourself a dead man." The city guards arrived. "What happened here?" the Captain demanded. Several people started talking at once. The Captain held his hand up for silence. "One at a time," he instructed.

"That man driving the wagon ran over this little girl," someone said. "And that man healed her!" another chimed in. Numerous people agreed. Broderick looked around, incredulous. "I didn't heal anyone," he said. "I heard the cracking of bone," said the first person. "And she was dead. She wasn't breathing," said another. The Captain didn't know what to make of the situation. "Take the driver into custody," he ordered one of his men. "Does the girl need medical attention?" he asked.

Derrick shook his head. "I will have my physicians look her over," he replied. The Captain nodded. "Very good. Everyone else, go about your business. You are blocking traffic."

The crowd seemed hesitant to disperse, but finally they went on their way. Derrick held his daughter's hand. "Broderick, my cousin! You will be staying with me at my estate," he announced. Broderick smiled. "You are too kind. But I will not be a burden on you."

"Nonsense," Derrick waved his hand. "Come now, you look like you could use a bath. And besides, I have some news for you." He smiled. Broderick always found it hard to tell his cousin no.

Derrick's home was more like a palace. When one had the money he did, anything one wanted could be had. Broderick had been there several times before and always found it to be a bit too much. What use did someone have for that many servants, anyway? His cousin's estate was located away from the hectic pace of the market area. It was situated on the top of a hill. Several roads led out from the house, some leading to the city and some to his honeysuckle farms.

Derrick's villa was a sprawling complex that consisted of four buildings. A smooth cobblestone path led to the large courtyard that sat in the middle of the multiplex. A single building sat on the north, east, and west sides of the courtyard, with the fourth building also on the west side though not as close to the main dwellings. The courtyard was decorated with statues of various mythical creatures, benches, and a fountain in the center.

The three buildings were connected to each other by beautiful gardens with sweet smelling flowers of all kinds. Each building looked exactly alike on the outside, though they all served a completely different purpose. The building to the north was the family dwelling, where Derrick and his wife and child lived. The building to the east was an oversized kitchen where one could find any variety of food available any time of the day. After sunset, the kitchen was free of servants, making it a self serve kitchen.

The building to the west was the servant quarters. Typically servants lived further from the main dwellings, but Derrick found the closer they were, the quicker it was to have their services. The fourth building, which was a couple hundred feet from the servant quarters, was where the harvested honeysuckle was brought and bottled. Derrick led Broderick up the stone path and through the courtyard into the main building. Broderick shook his head, as he did every time, when they stepped inside. They walked into a massive atrium. "You have too much money," Broderick said.

Derrick looked quizzically at his cousin and then smiled in understanding. "It is a popular design," he answered. "The space allows the house to be well lit and ventilated. I find the room to be quite useless, but my wife loves it. Ah, and here she is."

Claire ran over and sat with Octavia who was sitting on a stone bench looking at a myriad of colored flowers that rose out from the porcelain vase next to the bench. "Octavia, dear, you remember Broderick?"

Octavia turned and smiled at Broderick. "I remember. We are indebted to you for saving our daughter," she said. "Thank you." The last was spoken solemnly. "I can't imagine life without my dear Claire."

Broderick shrugged. "I didn't do anything, really. I just happened to be in the same part of town when I heard a scream. I had no idea what had happened. All I did was hold her in my arms. I thought she was …" his words broke and he had to pause to calm his quavering voice. "She was unharmed, for which I am thankful myself."

Claire turned her attention to Broderick. That same look he saw in the market shone in her eyes. It made him uncomfortable. Broderick turned his gaze to Octavia. "I hope I am not being a burden," he said, changing the subject.

Octavia laughed. "Oh please. You are family, Broderick. You are welcome here anytime." Derrick nodded his agreement. "Indeed cousin. Please, make yourself comfortable. The servants are preparing dinner as we speak."

Broderick felt like the term dinner was an understatement. Feast would have been more appropriate. The servants brought in fresh baked breads, soups of all kinds, a plate full of various cheeses, and bottles of the expensive honeysuckle. He ate and drank his fill and noticed the sun was beginning to set. The servants came through and lit candles, placing them around the atrium. Broderick yawned and stretched. He was much more tired than he thought.

Derrick noticed and knew his cousin was probably ready to rest. "Come outside with me," he said, motioning Broderick to follow him. They stepped out into the courtyard. The statues had an eerie appearance in the fading light. A gentle breeze stirred, reminding them that summer had yet to burn fiercely.

"I have a question, cousin."

Broderick nodded and told him to speak it. "In the market today … what the people said. Is it true?" Broderick seemed confused. "Is what true?"

"After the accident when the guards came. Some of the people said that you healed my daughter. Is it true?"

Broderick chuckled. "No, I am no healer. You should know that. People see what they want to see. Perhaps they wanted to see a miracle because Claire appeared to be hurt but really wasn't. I honestly don't know why anyone would think that."

Derrick nodded but wasn't convinced. "What about all the blood?" Broderick had thought of that, but didn't know how there could be blood when there was no wounds on the child. "Maybe it wasn't hers? I don't know that either." Both men remained silent for long moments.

"Well, I suppose it doesn't matter. Claire is fine and is as joyful as ever. I'm sure you would like to get some sleep." Derrick escorted Broderick back into the house and to a room located off the atrium. "You can use this room while you are here. And stay as long as you like. I don't know how you keep your sanity living in the woods alone. It's not normal, cousin." Derrick grinned.

Broderick playfully pushed his cousin out of the way and shut the door behind him. He pulled his shirt off and fell into the bed. It was softer and more comfortable than anything he had ever laid on. He rolled onto his back and stared up at the ceiling, going over their conversation. *Where had all that blood come from if not from Claire? And the look in her eyes ...*

Broderick shivered. As he was slowly drifting asleep, a sudden realization struck him. *The bird.*

Chapter 3

Broderick woke the next morning to the musical songs of birds. He stretched and sat up on the edge of the bed, his feet dangling above the floor. He had several weird dreams through the night. Birds and dead people following him. He ran from them, but he could never escape them.

He shook his head and had the feeling someone was staring at him. The door was cracked and he saw an eye staring through the door. "You can come in," he said. The door pushed open and Claire stood there. She smiled at him and entered sheepishly. "Did I wake you up, uncle?"

Broderick shook his head. "No, you didn't. What are you up to today?" he asked as he got off the bed and grabbed his shirt. He paused midway putting it on when she said, "I was watching you sleep." He pulled the shirt over his chest and looked at her. "That sounds boring."

She shook her head. "Not as boring as it sounds. Besides, when people sleep is when you get to see who they really are. And now I know."

"Know what?" he asked.

"Nothing," she said. She looked around and then whispered, "You brought me back." Then she turned and skipped out of the room. Broderick stared at where she stood for a moment before shaking his head and walking out into the atrium. The servants had already brought breakfast. Broderick was greeted by Derrick and Octavia. "She didn't wake you, did she?" Octavia asked, looking at Claire sternly.

"What? No," Broderick answered. He sat down with them. He ate biscuits covered with butter and several different kinds of berries. The flavors exploded in his mouth. He always found that things tasted so good in the morning. "Sleep well?" Derrick questioned. Broderick nodded because his mouth was full. He swallowed and drank some water. "I could certainly use a bed like that. It was like sleeping on a pile of baby chickens." They all laughed and continued eating.

A servant hurriedly walked in and approached Derrick, leaning down and whispering something in hushed tones. Derrick's eyes flickered to Broderick. "Where are the soldiers?" he asked the servant. He explained they were present but would probably be overwhelmed. "You may want to see it for yourself," the servant said. Derrick stood up. "Excuse me for a moment, dear," he said to Octavia. He followed the servant outside.

Broderick looked questioningly at her. "What's that about?" She shrugged and took a sip from her glass. "There's no telling. Sometimes the servants get injured fending off thieves in the fields. That's a possibility. Honeysuckle isn't cheap, you know." He nodded and finished his glass of water.

They sat in silence until Derrick came rushing back in. "Broderick," he said breathlessly. "Come with me." They left the building and passed through the courtyard, traveling down the cobblestone path toward the edge of his estate. A crowd of people were gathered at the gatehouse that led to Derrick's property. Most of the wealthier people had their own hired soldiers. Derrick's guarded the gates and paths into his property and patrolled his fields.

"What's going on?" Broderick asked. Derrick didn't answer. They reached the gatehouse and a cheer rang through the crowd. The guards had formed a wall with their bodies and were keeping the crowd from forcing their way through. When Broderick came into view, the multitude pressed harder, almost breaking through the soldiers' line. "Get back!" the captain yelled at them. "You are not allowed to enter here!"

Broderick looked to his cousin who merely shrugged. "It seems they are here to see you," he said. Broderick's face screwed up. "Me? Why?" Again he shrugged.

"Please sir," a woman begged. She stood outside the throng of people holding a small child in her arms. "Please help me! My baby is dying! Please!" Broderick walked to the gate and the woman held her child out toward him. "Please," she begged again. At the sight of Broderick coming near, the crowd calmed and stopped pressing against the soldiers. They all watched with rapt attention to see what would happen.

"I'm sorry," he said to her. "I think you have the wrong person." A man from the crowd objected. "That's him! I saw him bring the child in the market back from the dead. He has power over death!"

Broderick didn't know what to do. He wasn't a healer, he was a woodcutter. The woman was desperate, he could see that. *Desperate people don't listen to reason.* "I did not heal anyone or," he looked at the man in the crowd, "bring anyone back to life.

You are looking for something that does not exist. I am not a healer."

No one spoke and no one moved. They just stood there staring. "Please," the woman whimpered. Tears fell from her eyes and trickled down her face. Broderick looked at the child. The boy couldn't be more than eight, he guessed. There was a sickness about the boy. His skin was pale and gaunt. His eyes were sunken into his head and he stared lifelessly at nothing. His heart broke for the woman, but there was nothing he could do.

He almost denied the charges of being a healer again, but when he looked into the mother's face, he knew he couldn't. *I will prove I am not a healer,* he decided. He reached his hand through the gate and grabbed the child's hand. Nothing happened. "You see ... I am not a healer ..." he whispered. The mother stared at her child. It seemed to Broderick as if time had stopped. A pinkish color in the pigment of the child's skin suddenly appeared on his hand and slowly made its way up the boy's arm. The sick white color soon was gone, and the boy's skin looked healthy.

The boy's eyes fluttered and the life came back into them. He looked to Broderick. That same intelligent focus appeared in the child's eyes. The same as Claire. The same as the bird. Broderick jerked his hand away.

The mother's tears were different. They were no longer tears of sadness, but of joy. "Thank you," she said elatedly. "Thank you!" Panic gripped him. *What just happened?* He stepped back a few steps, shaking his head in disbelief. He bumped into Derrick and it startled him. He looked at his cousin and saw the wild look on his face reflected in Derrick's eyes. He turned and fled back to the villa.

He stumbled and almost tripped. He couldn't see straight. *I'm going crazy. I must be crazy.* His mind raced from the bird, to Claire, and then to the boy. The bird. Claire. The boy. Was it possible?

—

"Cousin," the voice sounded far away. Broderick found himself swimming in darkness. It was as though his eyes were closed and he couldn't open them. "Broderick." The voice was louder this time. He opened his mouth to speak. He felt his lips part but no sound came out.

A hand touched his shoulder and shook him. "Cousin." Broderick forced his eyes open and blinked several times. He saw Derrick staring down at him. "Are you okay?" he asked.

"What happened?" Broderick asked. Derrick helped him to his feet. "I think you passed out. I found you lying here in the courtyard." They stood staring at one another, neither man speaking. "I don't know what's happening," Broderick finally said. He related the story of his finding the rock that fell from the sky, the bird that seemed dead but wasn't, and the giant attack. Then the market when he came upon Claire. And now the boy.

"I do not have powers," Broderick declared. "I don't know what is happening, but I do not have powers." Derrick sat silent in thought. "Perhaps that's true," he said. "Perhaps it isn't you that has powers.

What if the stone you found has powers? You said it fell from the sky?" Broderick nodded.

"Who knows what it could be. But it seems that since you found it, all of these events have been happening. I think the answer to this mystery involves the stone. Where is it?" Broderick produced it from his belt and gave it to his cousin. Derrick looked it over but couldn't tell what it was. "We should take this to Torg. Maybe he will know what it is."

"I did take it to him," Broderick replied. "He said it was nothing but a pretty rock." Derrick tapped his chin. "Hmm. I may know someone else we can ask." He lowered his voice and looked around. Drawing closer to Broderick, he said, "Before I took up an honest trade, I used to dabble in some unseemly things with some … unscrupulous men."

Broderick raised his eyebrow. "What do you mean?" Derrick barely spoke above a whisper. "There is a man … at least, I think he is a man. He lives at the edge of the city near the slums. He is a wizard, but not like the wizards in Ravendale. He does things that aren't natural. Things banned by the Church. If anyone would know what that stone is, he would."

"Is it safe to go to this man?"

"Not right now," Derrick answered. "We will wait until nightfall, then we will go." Broderick nodded. "You never told me that," he said, looking his cousin in the eye.

"For good reason," his cousin responded.

"Why is that?"

Derrick hesitated. "He's a necromancer."

Chapter 4

The rest of the day passed without incident. The crowd at the gatehouse didn't leave, but they weren't trying to get past the soldiers now. Derrick doubled the number of the guards just to be safe. Broderick spent most of the day walking the honeysuckle fields and watching the servants harvest the nectar. His cousin had spent the majority of the day dealing with the various aspects of his business.

Broderick hoped this wizard fellow could tell him what the shard was and how it was causing odd things to happen. While he walked the fields, he did notice what appeared to be a figure among the tree line that bordered Derrick's fields. The figure was hidden among the shadows, so he couldn't make out any details. He looked to see where the nearest guard was to have him investigate it, but when he turned back the figure was gone.

He didn't see whoever it was again the rest of the day. After dinner, Derrick told his wife that he and Broderick would be back late in the night and not to wait up for him. Claire insisted on Broderick tucking her in before they left. Once they were gone, Derrick handed Broderick a dagger. "For safety," he insisted. "The slums are a dangerous place, especially for someone like me."

Broderick strapped the blade to his belt and hid it under his shirt. Broderick had been to Myrwood many times, but he had never been to the slums. Myrwood was an economic powerhouse and boasted one of the biggest workforces across Rundäë, but even so, many people still managed to fall through the cracks of such a rich society. Most of them lived in the slums. Abandoned warehouses and old shops that were no longer used served as homes for them. Thieves and murderers found shelter here as well. Everyone who called it home adhered to a strict code of honor. No one stole from another, and no one killed another.

Anyone who happened to accidentally wander into the slums, however, was fair game for anyone. Derrick and Broderick had dressed in the clothing of some of his servants. They weren't the tattered rags of the homeless, but Derrick assured his cousin that they would blend in enough to pass through unharmed. Broderick hoped his cousin was right.

The sky wasn't marred by a single cloud. The moon was full and bright, reflecting off the smooth stones that made up the roads through the city. They passed a few buildings that made Broderick assume they were in the derelict part of town. He couldn't have been more wrong. "These are just the middle class homes," Derrick informed him. Broderick began to dread seeing anything worse.

They left the paved roads and began traveling down dirt paths wide enough for three people side to side. Broderick doubted he would have felt any safer during the day. A stream ran through the town and they crossed over via an old and worn bridge. The streets didn't have lanterns lighting the way like the better areas of town. Here and there Broderick could make out bodies lying against the rickety buildings. He didn't know if they were dead or drunk.

The path they were on branched left and right. "Which way?" Broderick asked. "I'm not sure,"

Derrick answered. "You don't know? I thought you've been here before?" Derrick patted the air to calm his cousin. "I did jobs for him, I never said I met him."

The shadowy figures of a couple thugs detached from a nearby building. "You lost?" one of them asked. The moonlight glinted off the metal of a blade. "Of course not," Derrick answered. "We're going to speak to the Necromancer." The thugs halted uncertainly. "Why would you be looking for the Necromancer? Don't you know what happens to people who cross him?"

Derrick nodded. "We do, but we do what we must to survive." He winked at Broderick. "Which road can we find him on?" The thug who spoke pointed to the left. "That way. Don't say I didn't warn you, though." They melted back into the shadows. Broderick couldn't tell if they were gone or not.

Derrick led them down the left fork without speaking. They walked for close to twenty minutes before they came upon a small, one-story brick building. "This must be it," Derrick announced.

"How do you know?" Broderick asked. Derrick pointed to the path. "Because the road ends here." There were no windows. A single wooden door seemed to be the only entrance. Derrick knocked and waited for an answer. They could hear someone shuffling inside.

"What do you want?" a deep voice demanded.

"We need your help."

They could hear what sounded like a latch being unlocked and the door cracked open slightly. A milky white eye, devoid of any pupil, looked out. The moonlight reflected eerily from the eye. "Help for what?"

Broderick stepped forward. "I have some questions," he said. "Questions about this." He held the shard up for the eye to see. "What is it?" the voice hissed. Broderick shrugged. "I was hoping you could tell me."

The door swung open silently and an ugly figure stepped out. A tall man, bald and wrinkled, greeted them. Broderick saw the person's other eye was the same. He suspected the person was blind. "Go in," the figure bade, casting a wary glance up the dirt path. They quickly heeded the command. They entered to find the room well lit with candles. Twisted symbols were traced on the walls with a red flaky substance. The figure shut the door and locked it before turning to face them.

"Why do you think I can tell you what you possess?"

Derrick spoke up. "You are the Necromancer, aren't you? I did a few jobs for some men who worked for you some years ago. I knew if anyone could tell us, you could." The figure remained silent for a moment before walking over to a table covered with a variety of vials and bowls filled with different colored materials.

"How can you see?" Broderick asked. He immediately felt dumb for asking. He should have kept his mouth shut. The figure looked at him and smiled. "I see more than you do." The figure raised his hands up before his face and breathed into them. The ugly appearance faded away. The Necromancer wasn't a man, but a woman. An attractive woman. Flowing blonde hair spilled down her back, glowing with a soft sheen in the candlelight. Her skin was smooth and flawless, the color of bronze. Her eyes, however, remained empty pools of white.

"I thought the Necromancer was a man," Derrick breathed softly. She smiled. "Reputation is everything," she replied. "How many would come seeking to steal my secrets if they knew the Necromancer was merely a woman? But you are not here for that. Let me see the stone."

Broderick held it out to her. She took it in her hands and laid it upon the table. Retrieving a book from a shelf behind her, she opened it and flipped through the pages. "I have seen this material before," she explained. "It is rare and valued immensely by wizards. Where did you get it?" she questioned.

Broderick related his tale to her. "I have heard word of you whispered in the streets. A healer, some say. Others claim you are a messenger from God. But we know you are neither. I know exactly what this stone is." She continued flipping through the pages of the book, looking for a specific page. "Here it is," she said. She turned the book so they could see. Images were drawn on one page and words were written on the other.

"What do you know of the sun?" she asked. "Besides the obvious?"

"Nothing?"

She shook her head, frowning. "Long before the demons ravaged our world, long before there were kings or boundaries, our sun was dying. The creative power that forged it was failing. In those days, wizards could harness powerful magic. They could boil oceans, crack open the skies, command the elements. Several wizards from varying beliefs came together in an attempt to save the world. No one knew for certain what would happen if the sun died, but many speculated our world would not survive.

"They decided to make a new sun. One that would not fail nor grow weak. It would be powered by their magic. There were three Orders of sorcerers. The Order of Shadow, who studied the darker side of magic. The Order of the Upright, who believed magic should be used to better the lives of people. And the Order of Neutrality, who believed every mage chose to use their magic however they saw fit.

"Each Order worked upon a piece of rare crystal, imbuing it with powerful spells. They melded the pieces together and wove the magic into it. When our sun finally died and darkness fell over the earth, the wizards unleashed the new sun. It has been the source of life ever since. The secrets of the magic used were never recorded and as time passed, wizards lost the ability to control such magic. They are still powerful, do not mistake that. But on much smaller levels than when our sun was re-made."

She held it up in the light. "This must be a piece of the sun. This shard is why you have experienced the things you have. It uses your body as a means to channel the magic. You are very lucky. Or very cursed."

"Cursed? How could he be cursed with something so powerful? The power of this shard brought my daughter back from death. Someone who can control power like that could do anything," Derrick interjected.

"Precisely," the Necromancer said. "You will be the target of every wizard who knows you possess this. I saw it fall from the sky. I know I am not the only one who did. There are others," she shuddered, "who will not be stopped from finding it, that I can assure you. Word of your 'miracles' has traveled quickly in Myrwood. You are not safe."

"I have many guards," Derrick said, waving his hand. "We are safe." The Necromancer laughed. "Do not be foolish. There are some things that cannot be stopped by steel and strength."

"I have noticed something," Broderick finally spoke. "With the bird, Claire, and the sick boy. They all have this look in their eyes. Is there any significance to this?" The Necromancer tilted her head. "What do you mean?"

"I cannot describe it. It makes me uncomfortable, though. And I don't know why."

"I'm going to show you something. Do not be afraid," she said. She closed her eyes and began to chant softly. A form came walking into the room from a doorway neither man had noticed. It was a man. A very dead man. "This is the product of my magic," she explained. "I can animate the body, but there is no intelligence to speak of. Just the base instincts. They are good for labor, but cannot do anything that requires them to think. It is said that wizards used to be able to raise the dead, binding the spirit back into the body.

"Perhaps this is what the magic of the shard has done. But beware," she warned ominously, "they may not be who they seem. Magic is powerful, but it is not like the natural forces of creation. Life is never *fully* restored to the body. There may be consequences that you do not see immediately. Now you must go," she pointed towards the door. "One more thing," she added as an afterthought. "Unless you were born with the gift, the magic will drive you mad in the end."

They turned to leave. Broderick wasn't sure what to do with the shard. *What if something bad comes from using it?* When they got outside, Derrick turned to him. "Do you know what this means, cousin? You could be king, if you wanted. People will worship you. Anything you want could be yours," Derrick spoke excitedly. "This is a blessing!"

Broderick pictured the look in the eyes of the bird, Claire, and the boy. He wasn't so sure his cousin was right.

Chapter 5

Broderick spent the trip back to his cousin's estate in silent contemplation. Derrick was going on about riches and popularity. Was that really what he wanted? Broderick didn't know what he wanted. He thought of the people that lived in the slums. Homeless, destitute, starving … and no one cared for them.

What if he could use the power of the shard for good? The words of the Necromancer echoed in his head. *It will drive you mad in the end.* Broderick was no sorcerer. Neither were his parents, nor anyone else in his family that he knew of. He shrugged that thought away and realized they were almost at Derrick's property. The crowd of people had still not dispersed, but seemed to be growing.

"I left orders with my guards to sneak us through a different way. I had a feeling this would happen," he nodded toward the people at his gates. Broderick didn't answer. He followed his cousin's lead, sliding through a space in the fence that was concealed by a some shrubbery. "These people are looking for something," Broderick said absently. Derrick smiled. "A hero," he answered. Broderick shook his head. "No. More than a hero. They are looking for a savior. A miracle worker."

The two exchanged looks. "That's what the Church is for," Derrick remarked. "Raven is the one who sacrificed his life to save the world from the demon horde."

"I know," Broderick said. "Yet the priests do not help the needy. They do not feed the hungry. They build up wealth and for what? Their own greed?" Broderick snorted derisively. "The power of their message is drowned out by their actions. These people need help. And if no one will do it, I will."

Derrick stopped walking and turned to his cousin. "You are a good man. I know your parents raised you to be that way. But you are thinking too small. You should aspire higher, Broderick. You could rule the land with that power. Why waste it helping people who don't help themselves?"

"Perhaps they can't help themselves," Broderick answered. "I have made my decision. I'm going to help them. I don't want to endanger you and your family, though." Derrick laughed. "Endanger my family? How so?"

"You heard what the Necromancer said. I am a target for people who know what I have."

Derrick shook his head. "She's just trying to scare you. She wants that rock, I could see it in her eyes. I have plenty of guards to keep us safe," he assured his cousin. "You are staying with me."

They made their way to the villa in silence, not wanting to wake Claire or Octavia. The door was slightly ajar, but Derrick wasn't concerned. They stepped into the atrium and found it a wreck. The flowers had been trampled and things had been knocked over. "What the hell happened here?" Derrick demanded angrily. "Octavia! Claire!" There was no answer from either. Broderick's heart jumped down into his stomach. He had a sick feeling that whatever happened was because of him.

Derrick went to find his wife, and Broderick went to look for Claire. He found her hiding in his room. "What happened?" he asked. Derrick came into the room in a panic. "I can't find Octavia. Claire!" He swept her up into his arms and clutched her tight. "Where is your mother?" he asked.

"They took her," she answered. Derrick set her down and kneeled down to look her in the face. "Who took her?"

"Strange men. They wore all black and tried to catch us both. I ran and hid in here, but they took mommy. She was screaming and tried to fight them. I was scared, daddy." Tears filled her eyes.

Derrick hugged her again. "We will find her, don't you worry." He had one of the servants stay with Claire while he questioned the captain of his guards. Broderick looked through the wreckage in the atrium for any clue as to who took Octavia and where she might be. "She must have put up quite a fight," he muttered to himself. The table and benches where they normally ate their meals at were knocked over. Freshly picked fruits littered the floor. A bottle of honeysuckle had shattered and broken glass was everywhere. A servant came scurrying into the atrium and began to clean up the mess.

"You didn't hear anything?" Broderick asked the young girl. She looked to him and shook her head. Broderick grunted in disbelief. *How did no one see or hear anything?* Derrick strode into the atrium from outside. "The guards didn't see anything. The Captain said there was nothing out of the ordinary. This doesn't make any sense. Where is my wife?" Broderick sighed. There had to be some clue.

"My lord," the servant girl said. She lifted a piece of parchment up. It was soaked with honeysuckle, but the ink had not run. Derrick hastily grabbed the letter and read it. "What does it say?" Broderick asked. Derrick handed it to him. Broderick read it twice. "How far is Ravendale from here?" he asked.

"A week's ride south," his cousin answered. "Who would have taken her, and why would they take her there?"

"I don't know the answer to that, but I will find her and bring her back."

"I'm coming with you," Derrick said. Broderick shook his head. "You can't. What about your daughter? What if those men come back? And who would run your farm?" Derrick waved that all away. "None of that matters. My wife has been kidnapped. You think I'm going to stay here and twiddle my thumbs?"

"No, I think you are going to stay here and protect your daughter and continue overseeing your business. I will go alone and bring her back safely. I promise."

"That is a horrible plan," a voice from the door said. They both turned to see the Necromancer standing there. The captain of the guards stood beside her. "She requested to see you. I would have turned her away, but she said it was important."

Derrick nodded and dismissed him. "What are you doing here?" he demanded of the Necromancer. She smiled at him. "Word travels quickly in my circles. Your wife is missing?"

Derrick didn't answer. "Yes," it was Broderick who spoke. "She was kidnapped and whoever took her left this note. It says they want the shard and to bring it to Ravendale. I'm going to get her and bring her back."

"You're either extremely brave or a complete fool. Personally I think it's a little of both," she said tersely. Broderick took the insult in stride. "What makes you say that?" he asked.

"You don't know, do you? Ravendale is a holy city, protected by warrior priests and a shield of magic that keeps out anyone the priests don't want coming in. And you think you can go alone?" she laughed.

"I can spare some of my guards," Derrick said. Broderick was shaking his head before his cousin finished the sentence. "No, it will be easier to go undetected without them."

"You don't seem to understand the gravity of this situation," the Necromancer interrupted. "You cannot just walk into the city. And *if* they let you in, how are you going to bring his wife back? You are really going to give up that rock?"

Broderick thought about it. "Then what?" he asked. "I'm coming with you," she retorted, as if that answered everything. Derrick raised his hands up. "Wait. You aren't going anywhere with him."

The Necromancer eyed him dangerously. "It would be bad for you if word got out about the work you used to do," she said. "Some of the things that happened by your hand." She let that sink in. He wouldn't want his reputation damaged. Derrick sighed in defeat. "Cousin, she has to go with you." Broderick shrugged. "We leave at daylight," she informed him.

"That's in an hour," Broderick protested. She smirked at him, her white eyes like two moons shining from her head. "I know."

Chapter 6

Broderick rode beside the Necromancer. She knew the way and so he was resigned to just following her lead. He had wanted to retrieve his own horses, but she said they would need a faster way of getting to Ravendale. "These horses are for work, we need some for traveling," she had informed him.

He didn't think it mattered as long as they were on the road. The stables where he had dropped off his wagon also had horses for sale. When he attempted to pay, the stable master refused payment. "I heard what you did for that sick boy," he said with a smile. "It's my honor to help you." Broderick wasn't prone to getting attention from anyone other than beautiful ladies. His blonde hair and green eyes were enough to drive a woman mad with lust, but add into that equation his well muscled body from hard labor … he was lucky to keep their hands off him most times.

They traveled in silence most of the day. Broderick didn't mind. He found the Necromancer to be an oddity. If it weren't for her peculiar eyes, he might almost find her attractive. Eventually curiosity got the better of him and he began talking to her. "What happened to your eyes?"

She didn't bother looking at him. "Why must you know?" she asked, keeping her gaze ahead. They were several hours away from Myrwood now, with only the occasional small farming community to pass through. "I don't have to know if you don't want to talk about it. When we first met, I thought you were blind. That's obviously not the case."

"When I first summoned a *balor*, I was a novice in my arts. It used its magic to sear my eyes. Eventually my sight returned. Most of it, anyway." She talked about it so casually that Broderick wondered where she got her internal strength from. "What is a balor?" he asked.

"A powerful demon," she answered. "Very tall and massive. I was lucky to dismiss it before it killed me." She remained silent, and Broderick thought he saw a pained look cross her features. It was fleeting, and he almost doubted that he even saw it. "People call you the Necromancer. Do you have a real name?" he inquired. She scowled at him. "Names are powerful, more than most realize. My name is my own and if I feel it is necessary to share it with you, I will. Until then, just call me Necromancer."

"Sorry," he said glumly. He stared out at the countryside and realized it was nearing dark. The sun was beginning to set and the sky took on an almost surreal look. Small wisps of cloud were scattered about, bathed in oranges and reds. The day had been comfortably warm and Broderick was beginning to feel the effects of not sleeping the night before. "We should find someplace to sleep," he remarked. "Before it gets too dark to see anything."

She nodded in agreement. There were hills nearby and Broderick could see the dark openings of caves. "There," he pointed. "Caves make good shelter if it rains, trust me." He chuckled at a distant memory. The Necromancer was not amused. "No, we will stay in the open. There are no rain clouds. And there's something about those caves I don't like."

Broderick sighed. She was a difficult one. He learned quickly it was pointless to argue with her. He didn't pack much as he was in a hurry to retrieve his cousin's wife. It was his fault she had been endangered. He pulled the shard from the pouch on his belt. It had brought him a lot of stress lately. He was of a mind to give it away to ensure he got Octavia back to Derrick safely. It was the least he could do.

He put the shard back and they stopped their horses. Broderick dismounted and pulled a blanket out of the saddle. He unrolled it and laid it on the ground. Leading the horse by the reins to a large dead tree, he wrapped them around a low hanging branch. There was plenty of grass to graze on. He pulled the xiphos his cousin had given him from the saddle and unsheathed it as he lay on his makeshift bed.

Daylight was slowly fading but he could still make out the details of the blade. It was a double-edged sword. It was light, well balanced, and intended to be wielded one handedly. The metal of the blade was silver in color, but Broderick didn't know what it was made of. Etched down the center of the blade were many runes. He couldn't read any of them. Near the hilt of the blade there was a single word in the common tongue. It read, "Sorandra".

The hilt was wood; a deep gray speckled with black. Broderick had seen trees with that odd coloring in the woods around his home. When he asked his cousin where he had gotten such a beautiful weapon, his cousin said it had been in the family for years. He sheathed the weapon and looked to see what the Necromancer was doing. She had tied her horse beside his and also made a bed out of a single blanket. Her back was to him. He thought about attempting to talk to her some more, but decided he was too tired.

His eyes were heavy and he was having trouble keeping them open. Sleep took him quickly.

—

The Necromancer waited until she knew Broderick was asleep. The night was silent and she heard his breathing slow. She got up and grabbed a sack from the saddle of her horse. She walked around the other side of the tree and lay the bag down. She crept silently over to where Broderick was sleeping. She watched his chest move up and down rhythmically. Kneeling down she withdrew the shard from his pouch. He didn't move. She walked back over to the tree.

She gathered a couple of sticks and set them in a pile then placed a handful of dry grass onto the sticks. Opening the sack, she withdrew a piece of firestone. It was gray and one side had a sharp, acute edge. She pulled a dagger from her boot and stuck the blade into one of the sticks. With her other hand, she began rubbing the firestone against the blade until it heated up. After several strikes, sparks began to fly off the steel. She watched until the sparks hit the grass and it began to smoke.

She leaned down and blew gently. A fire sprang to life, igniting the kindling. She quickly added more grass and sat back. She hadn't lit the fire for warmth, for it was almost summer and the air was temperate and slightly humid. She watched as the flames consumed the sticks and began a small fire. She reached into the folds of her robes and pulled out a small bag containing black powder. She opened it and sprinkled a few grains into the fire. The flames danced wildly. She weaved her hands over the fire and began to chant softly.

The flames swayed with the motions of her hands. "Skiram," she called. The flames began to change color. She repeated the name two more times. The flames roared up and took the shape of a face. "Skiram," she breathed, "Lord of the Flame." She prostrated herself before the fiery face.

"Rise," a voice said from within the fire. She lifted her head. "Tell me, Necromancer, why do you summon me?" She had been confident until this moment. Skiram was a demon. He was known as the Lord of the Flame for he could only be summoned through the element of fire. He was also a master of deceit. She took care when dealing with him.

"I have summoned you to ask a favor, Lord." The face in the flames remained emotionless. She swallowed hard. She had been summoning other worldly creatures for years, but Skiram was different. He was powerful, ruthless, and clever. He had tricked her once before, and she refused to be tricked by the demon again.

"I'm listening," Skiram said. The Necromancer cleared her throat before she spoke. "You know what I seek and why I seek it," she began. Skiram interrupted her. "I have told you before, I have no power over this matter. Their strength comes from one greater than I."

She nodded and tried to be patient. "I know this, Lord. I do not need your help with that. I have something in my possession to handle that." She displayed the shard to the fiery face. Skiram's eyebrows rose; the demon was impressed. "Ancient magic," he said. "I feel it pulsing in your hand. How did you come by it?"

She smirked. "That is my secret to keep. What I need is much easier for you, but impossible for me." She laid out her plot in detail, explaining why she needed what she asked of him. Skiram's fiery appearance grinned and once he even laughed wickedly. The Necromancer peered through the tree branches to make sure the sound didn't wake Broderick. She was relieved to see he hadn't moved.

"I will grant you what you ask, but you must do something for me." She figured as much and was prepared to hear the worst. "I require a sacrifice."

She nodded her head. "An animal?" she asked. Many demons asked for animal sacrifices, but she had yet to discover the reason. "I am not some lesser spirit who plays god over barbarian tribes," Skiram spat. "I will demand my sacrifice when I choose, and it will be whatever I choose. You will be bound to honor your vow."

She considered his words. Aside from her craft, she didn't have much to lose. A petty sacrifice seemed fair. She was getting the better end of this deal by far. "I agree," she finally said. "Reach into the flames," Skiram commanded. She obeyed and felt the heat of the fire scorch her flesh. She gasped but kept her hand engulfed until Skiram told her to remove it.

A rune of binding was burned into her palm. "To ensure your end of the bargain," the demon told her. She bit her lip against the searing pain and bowed her head. The flames roared up and then went out completely, leaving her temporarily blinded in the dark. She sheathed the dagger back into her boot and replaced everything she had taken from the bag back inside.

The Necromancer laced her sack back onto her saddle and was about to lie down to rest when she heard the snapping of a twig. She froze and looked around. Her eyes had yet to readjust to the darkness, but she could see Broderick was still sleeping. She thought it may have been a wild animal. After several moments of silence, she decided it was safe and relaxed upon the blanket she had laid out. *Everything is coming together.* She closed her eyes to get some sleep.

Broderick rolled onto his side and woke up, feeling a rock jabbing him from under the blanket. He grunted and blearily slid his hand under the blanket and removed the rock. He heard a sound that gave him pause. He waited and listened to see if he heard it again. Hearing nothing, he was about to go back to sleep when he heard the unmistakable sound of a voice. He looked over at the Necromancer but it seemed to him that she was asleep.

He unconsciously held his breath and waited. There it was again. He could hear voices, but they did not speak any language he had heard before. It was guttural and sounded like someone trying to clear their throat. And then he saw them. About six small shadows quietly approaching. He slowly wrapped his hand around the hilt of his sword.

The moon shone bright and when the small forms stepped out of the shadows, Broderick involuntarily sucked in his breath.

Goblins!

Standing between three to three and a half feet tall, they were not an impressive sight. Their skin color usually ranged from a sickly yellow to a deep red. Most goblins didn't weigh more than fifty pounds. Though they were small and light, their strength was startling. A single goblin could rip the limbs off a trained soldier in full armor. From his view, Broderick could see they were all wearing brown colored leather, most likely mismatched armor scavenged from their victims.

Goblins favored ambushes. Broderick cursed himself for a fool. They should have checked the caves. They were sneaking up on the Necromancer. He could see the glint of metal in their hands. Six armed goblins against him and a woman. He had a sword and was versed enough in its use to hold his own, but what about her? Not having time to formulate a plan, he leapt up and unsheathed his sword.

The goblins halted. A man carrying a sword apparently caused them to second guess themselves. They all looked to the same goblin whom Broderick guessed was their leader. The creature snarled an order and they began moving toward him. The leader held up a serrated blade and continued stalking toward the Necromancer.

"Wake up!" Broderick shouted. But the Necromancer wasn't there. The goblin seemed just as surprised as Broderick. She appeared behind the leader and pressed her dagger to his throat. Her white eyes shone dangerously and she drove the blade into the creature's flesh. A gurgling sound escaped the goblin's mouth before she pushed him to the ground.

Broderick leapt forward and thrust his blade straight ahead at the nearest goblin. He managed to nick it in the shoulder. The others fanned out around him. Goblins are cowardly by nature, but when numbers are on their side, they are able to take down most enemies. Broderick held his sword out before him, slapping aside the goblins' attempts to strike him. It was only a matter of time before they got the idea to rush him. He risked a glance to the Necromancer and saw her drawing in the dirt.

Well she wasn't much help. He blocked another strike from a goblin and rushed the creature, swinging a wide arc to try to cut his head off. The goblin back-pedaled, tripped, and fell onto its back. Broderick twisted the hilt in his hand and drove the blade down into the creature's stomach. It howled in pain and thrashed about. He twisted the blade and turned in time to see a goblin fist crash into the side of his face.

His vision blurred momentarily. *They're stronger than they look!* That moment was all they needed. They howled with fury and rushed him. He went down under a mass of goblin flesh. He punched and kicked in a desperate attempt to get them off, all to no avail. His muscles were burning from the effort. His chest was heaving as he tried to breath.

Suddenly the weight atop him felt lighter. One after another the goblins were pulled off. He struggled to his feet and picked up his sword which had fallen out of his grasp. A decomposed corpse was fighting the goblins. He didn't have time to question what was happening, for one of the goblins was running toward the Necromancer. Broderick forced his feet to obey him and ran after the creature. He yelled a warning but she didn't seem to hear him. She appeared to be in some sort of trance.

The goblin raised its wicked looking blade and was about to drive it into her but Broderick lunged forward and threw himself bodily into the small creature. They crashed to the ground in a heap of thrashing fists. The goblin bit his hand that held the sword. The pain caused him to jerk his hand back and drop his sword. The goblin punched him in the nose and rose up quickly, trying once again to stab the Necromancer. Broderick rolled onto his side and tripped the goblin with his foot. He compelled his muscles to continue working and grabbed his sword, rising and moving to stand protectively in front of the woman.

Another goblin broke free of the fight with the corpse and came running, swinging its curved sword wildly. Broderick parried several swings but had forgotten the other goblin. Sharp, agonizing pain shot up his left arm. He saw he had inadvertently stepped back into the other goblin's swing, unknowingly saving the life of the Necromancer.

His anger burned through the pain and he lashed out with his foot, kicking the goblin that stabbed him in the groin. The creature crumbled to the ground, clutching itself. He turned back expecting to be assailed by the other goblin. They had all taken flight. The walking corpse had killed one and left another seriously injured. It lay in a puddle of its own blood, clutching a wound that kept bleeding.

"Cowards," he grunted. The corpse disintegrated into dust before his eyes and he turned to see the Necromancer looking at him with a concerned look on her face. "You're bleeding," she said. He shrugged. "It's nothing. I've done worse to myself with an ax and a tree," he laughed. For all his bluster, the pain was excruciating.

She didn't press the issue. "You saved my life," she said instead. "Thank you."

"I stepped into the blow accidentally," he responded grimly. "Not saying I wouldn't have done it intentionally, though." She stepped close and looked at his arm. "I should treat it anyway. Goblin blades are usually dipped in poison."

"We don't have time," he replied. He slid the blade into his belt and wrapped his hand around the wound. "They are gone now, but they'll be back with more of their kind." She waved away his words. "We will make time." She led him to the horses and retrieved her bag. She withdrew a few long, slender leaves that smelled strongly of mint. "What is that?" Broderick asked.

"Wintergreen," she answered. "Also known as King's Cure." She put one of the leaves into her mouth and chewed it up. She spit it into her hand and told him to move his hand. She wiped the wound with the cuff of her robes and applied the chewed leaf onto his wound. She repeated this until his wound was covered.

To Broderick's surprise, the leaves didn't sting his flesh. If anything, he felt as though they were lessening the burning in his arm. "Thanks," he said, looking over her work before she wrapped his arm up.

"It's nothing," she said with a smile. He untied the reins of his horse. "We should get moving before the goblins decide to come back."

When the goblins returned with reinforcements, they found the campsite long abandoned.

Chapter 7

They rode until the horses tired out. Broderick hadn't slept much before they had been attacked by the goblins and was finding it hard to stay awake. It didn't take much to convince the Necromancer that they needed to find somewhere safe with a comfortable bed to rest.

They stopped at one of the farms they passed and were able to feed and water their horses for a small price. After seeing to the horses, they slept in one of the barns. When Broderick awoke, the sky had already went dark. He didn't see the Necromancer anywhere. *Perhaps she is already awake.* He stretched and left the barn to see what food could be found. The Necromancer was carrying two bowls and he almost bumped into her. "I'm sorry," he said, putting a hand on her shoulder to steady her.

"It's okay," she replied, smiling. He quickly removed his hand. "What's this?" he asked, nodding at the bowls. "Dinner. Our host has heard word of the 'blonde man who performs miracles.'"

Broderick shook his head. He accepted the bowl she handed to him and then used some logs to create some crude seats. Lanterns hung at spaced intervals on the barn and lit up the area around them. The owner of the farm had treated them to some sort of breaded chicken. They ate in silence for long moments before the Necromancer spoke. "You and your cousin must be close."

Broderick had to finish chewing before he could answer. "We grew up together. My parents owned land near the mountains and we all lived there. His family eventually moved to Myrwood. We still saw each other, but not as often. When my parents died, he helped me continue working with lumber," Broderick smiled as the memories flooded him. "That's why I will do whatever I can to help him. That's what family does."

The Necromancer frowned but didn't say anything. "What about you?" he asked her. She stared out in the distance, seeing something he couldn't imagine. "I don't have any family," she said softly. She cleared her throat and finished her food, then she rose and walked back into the barn. Broderick finished his meal and stared up at the stars. They were scattered across the sky like tiny lanterns floating on a black sea.

He thought about the Necromancer. What was her real name? Why did she seem so guarded? He could only guess. He didn't know what to do with his bowl so he left it on the logs and went inside the barn. He found the Necromancer sleeping. They had made their beds out of big piles of straw. Her blanket lay at her feet. Her robes had parted slightly down the middle and he could almost glimpse her nakedness. He grabbed the blanket and gently placed it over her then went back outside.

The air was warm but not uncomfortable. He grabbed one of the lanterns and went for a walk. He walked along the perimeter of the fields. Tall green stalks rose up from the ground and he could see the corn was almost ready to be harvested. Broderick walked for a long distance around the fields, hoping it would tire him enough to sleep. He was wide awake and didn't want to mix up his days and nights. He eventually decided it was no use and turned back. He could see the light of the lanterns shining brightly. The light moved about wildly and reminded him of a large fire he had once seen … and then he realized he didn't see lanterns. He saw …

Fire.

He sprinted toward the barn, his legs pumping furiously. He tossed the lantern aside, realizing it was only hindering him. He arrived back at the barn to find it ablaze. He could hear screaming coming from the main dwelling. He hoped the Necromancer had gotten out, but the searing heat kept him from being able to check. He ran over to the stables and retrieved his sword from the saddle. It was hanging on a hook from the wall. He brandished the weapon and ran toward the house of the farmer. He unexpectedly found a band of goblins pillaging the house.

They must have followed us! He cursed and ran inside the house, cutting down two goblins who weren't paying any attention. He saw several more tearing things apart. It appeared they were searching for something. He heard screams coming from the upper level of the house. He climbed the stairs two at a time. He was breathing furiously, almost gasping aloud. He kicked open a door just in time to see a goblin hack off a young girl's arm.

Her scream turned into a gurgle of pain. Broderick could tell by the blood flowing that she wouldn't make it. But that didn't stop him from slashing the ugly creature to pieces. He searched the other rooms but found the rest of the family had met a similar fate. Tears stung his eyes as he fled back down the stairs. *This is our fault.* He blamed himself. If he hadn't of wanted to stop, the goblins would never have stopped here.

He got outside and found the fire had spread from the barn to the fields and was quickly racing toward the house. The stables were attached to the house. Once the fires reached the house, it wouldn't be long before they burned the stables also. Broderick killed another goblin, this one alone, before he ran into the stable to get his horse. He noticed that the other horse, the Necromancer's, was nowhere to be found. "Where would she have gone?" he muttered to himself.

His eyes widened when he thought of her warning, that he was a target for anyone who knew he had the shard. He searched the pouches on his belt in a panic. It was gone. He should have known. He didn't have time to dwell of the betrayal.

He mounted his horse and rode out of the stable. Flames were licking the sides of the house now, seeking to devour everything in its path. He steered his horse toward the road, determined to rescue Octavia whether he had the shard or not. He looked over his shoulder and saw the goblins had taken note of his flight. He urged the horse to speed up. He was far away from the farm before he finally allowed the horse to slow its pace. There was nothing in sight. The stars gave him enough light to see a few feet ahead of him, but nothing more. He shook his head in despair. Those people had died needlessly.

"Don't blame yourself," a familiar voice echoed in the night. He snapped his gaze toward the sound. The Necromancer, astride her horse, came riding to meet him from behind. "I know that you think it is your fault that that family is dead," she said, slowing her horse to ride beside him.

"Where were you?" he asked suspiciously. "And I know you took it!" Her face showed no emotion. "I was looking for you. When I heard the goblins attacking, I snuck into the stable and got my horse. I had no idea where you had went, so I rode around the house and toward the fields. When I didn't find you, I feared they had killed you." She sighed and extended her hand.

The starlight glinted off the smooth edges of the shard. "It fell out of your pouch while you slept," she lied. "I didn't want to wake you, so I held onto it to keep it safe. I forgot to give it to you when you woke up." She continued holding it out to him until he took it.

"You forgot?" he said, the sarcasm in his tone obvious. She nodded her head. "If I wanted the shard, I could easily have had it when you and your cousin came to me with it," she said.

"Why didn't you?" he asked.

"I have no need of it," she answered.

—

The sun came up a few hours later, painting the sky with bright colors. They hadn't talked much. Broderick was still grieving over the dead family. The Necromancer was thinking about her deal with Skiram. Her anger and hatred was strong. She weighed the effects of what her actions would cause.

Was it worth the cost? She used to think so. Now? Now she wasn't so sure. She wanted the justice that no one gave her. But she wasn't sure she could go through with it.

She sighed and looked over at Broderick. He was handsome, with his blonde hair and green eyes. She could lose herself in his gaze. She had begun to imagine what his muscular body would feel like pressed against hers. She never really wanted a relationship, choosing instead to study her craft and gain power. She had found herself immediately attracted to Broderick when he first brought the shard to her. She had dismissed it, seeing her attraction as weakness. When her plan began to formulate, however, she knew she would have to travel with him.

She wanted to hate him. It would make her task so much easier to hate him. But she couldn't. Broderick was so charming. And he had saved her life. Inadvertently, true, but he had stepped into the blow that would have killed her. She owed him.

"Kira," she said. Broderick looked up, startled at the unexpected sound of her voice. "What?"

"My name. It's Kira." Broderick stared at her for a moment and then smiled. "What made you tell me?" he asked. She looked away to hide her embarrassment. "You saved my life," she answered. "I owe you that much at least."

"It is a pretty name. Why don't you use it more?" Broderick flashed a smile at her, the first she had seen since the goblin attack at the farm. She turned her eyes forward before she answered him. "I find my identity in my title. The Necromancer is not just something that describes what I do, it is who I am. I crave power. The magic is a means to an end for me."

"What end is that?" he asked curiously.

She glowered. Gods how she wanted to hate him. "Nevermind," she said harshly. Broderick didn't press her further, for which she was thankful. "Why did you come with me?" he questioned.

"I told you at your cousin's estate why I was coming. You can't expect to just walk into Ravendale."

"I know that. But what did you feel you owed me to come along?"

She sighed with impatience. "I have something I've been meaning to do there, and this just seemed like the perfect time to do it. I don't feel like I owe you anything. In fact, it will be *you* who owes *me* after all this."

Broderick laughed, but he didn't think she was kidding. She would require something from him. *We'll cross that bridge when we get to it.*

The goblins managed to find them each night. And each night, Broderick and Kira fled before them. The next four days were no different.

Chapter 8

"Gaetano is dying," Justus said somberly. A great murmur ran through the gathering of priests. "This is a sad time for us, but we must hold off on our grieving. This council must vote a new leader. As we all know, there are many pressing matters that cannot be ignored. Morell and Rainor are well known among all of you. We will take the day to deliberate between the two and convene tomorrow. You are dismissed."

Everyone except Justus and Morell left. The two sat in silence until the room was completely empty and Justus made sure there wasn't anyone hanging around in the hallway. "You know this will be a difficult vote for the council," Justus remarked. Morell shrugged. "I do not think so."

The council room was large but plain. A long rectangular table sat in the middle of the room. Each side of the table had ten chairs, and only one end of the table had a chair. The end chair was specifically for the council leader of the warrior-priests. It had remained empty during the meeting. Justus was the right hand to Gaetano, the current leader. While he did lead the council temporarily, the candidates were chosen based upon their deeds of bravery and generosity. Justus was ineligible as he was not a noble by birth.

"Rainor sides with Gaetano on almost every issue," Justus reminded. "The men of the council believe Gaetano is second only to the blessed Raven in wisdom."

"Gaetano is an old fool," Morell said disdainfully. "And so is anyone who follows him. The church has grown weak with his leadership. The people do not respect us as they once did. The church coffers are bordering on empty. And why? Because Gaetano believes we should merely give it all away." He snorted derisively. "I will make us great again."

Justus smiled. "You speak with such passion! I believe you can do what you say. The others, however," Justus waved his hand about, "… they are ignorant sheep who do not like change. I think you will be hard pressed to beat out Rainor with your visionary changes."

Morell tapped his finger on the table contemplatively. "Unless Rainor wasn't in the running." Justus looked confused. "How would he not be?"

"Accidents happen all the time, especially in the field," Morell answered. Justus was aghast. "Do not speak such wickedness!" He made a motion in the air with his hand, one that was a common sign of warding off evil. Morell laughed.

"I was jesting with you, my friend. I would never think of such a thing. Besides, I would need him at my side as Gaetano has needed you all these years. I will just have to show the council that I am more qualified. A simple task." Morell rose from his chair. "I must leave you now. I have several matters that demand my attention. I will see you in the morning at the meeting."

Justus nodded and he took his leave. Morell cursed Justus as he navigated his way through the corridors. The man was so righteous minded it drove

Morell crazy. Once he entered his personal chambers, he removed his ceremonial robes that represented his status as a member of the council and hung them up on a hook.

He entered his washing room. A small table sat against the far wall. A silver bowl filled with fresh water sat atop it as well as a neatly folded towel. Morell walked over and splashed the water on his face, rubbing it furiously over his skin. He dried his face with the towel and looked into the mirror that hung on the wall.

His eyes were a steel grey color. He kept his hair short. Once a deep black, it was now being invaded by white. It seemed as though every time he had it cut, more white took over. Small lines from age scattered across his face, giving others a reasonable guess as to his age.

While almost everyone in Ravendale knew him as a warrior-priest of the church, he was far from being blameless. His rise to the council had been accomplished through deceit and several murders. He never personally got his hands dirty. At least, not anymore. It was always much easier to hire some criminal to do the deeds for him.

His rise had almost ended badly. His wife had caught him with a whore from the streets and had threatened to tell the council. He couldn't have allowed her to do that, of course. And so he had strangled her. And his daughter witnessed the entire thing. Now that had been a hard decision. Looking back and considering all he had gained, he would have gladly burned her eyes out again if he had to.

He pushed the memories back behind their wall and considered how he could rid himself of Rainor. He could hire someone to pay him a visit, but it seemed too risky. Perhaps he could find some way to push the council meeting back?

Morell growled in frustration and left the washing room. He threw himself into a chair and rubbed his temples. He had to figure out *something*.

Chapter 9

Broderick was exhausted. The constant traveling with only an occasional stop over the last few days was taking its toll. Their mounts trotted along at an easy pace. It was hard for him to enjoy the scenery. It was even harder to keep his eyes open. He looked at Kira to see how she was faring. If she was tired, it didn't show.

"We should reach Ravendale late tonight, possibly early in the morning." Broderick had grown accustomed to her voice. She was demanding and strong willed. Her milky white eyes, which had first unnerved him, now gave him a longing that he found thrilling. He didn't know if she felt the same, but he hoped that their path together did not end at Ravendale.

Their horses were just as exhausted as they were and they were not able to make it to the city limits before having to stop. They set up camp but decided not to set a watch this night. They were close enough to the city that armed patrols would spot the goblins that had been following them if they dared to come near. They ate what little remained of their provisions, which consisted of some bread that had started to go stale, and some apples.

When they got ready to go to sleep, Kira made her bed startlingly close to his. He didn't say anything, choosing instead to watch her wordlessly. He finally lay down and stared up at the sky. Now that he was able to go to sleep, he found it eluding him. He cursed his mind for keeping him awake.

"Do you think I am pretty?"

Kira's voice startled him. He thought she had fallen asleep already. His heart battled his mind for what felt like hours. Should he answer honestly? What if she was using him? What is she wasn't?

"I think you are beautiful," he said finally, hesitantly. He thought he could see her smile. "I must admit, you have really grown on me."

Kira's heart soared. Could someone really care for her? She kept reminding herself that he had saved her life. Not just anyone would do that. She moved her bed next to his and lay down, facing him.

They stared at each other for long moments. She leaned over slowly, her body trembling. Their lips met and fire burned through Broderick's body. Their kissing became more passionate, and his hands began to explore her body. He opened her robes and found to his delight that she wore a shift. The material was so sheer it essentially revealed everything. *No wonder she wears robes.*

His left hand wandered between her thighs. She gasped in pleasure. She quickly removed the shift, revealing the glory of her body to him in full. His breathing was quick and shallow. He allowed her to remove his clothing as well. She pushed him down and straddled him. "I hope you are ready for this," she whispered.

—

Dawn came all too quick. Broderick woke up, the sun shining on his face. He rolled over and found Kira still sleeping. She was dressed, which made him pause to wonder if perhaps he had dreamed it all. Looking under his blanket revealed that it was no dream.

He got up and clothed himself. With the sun shining, he could clearly see Ravendale in the distance. He left the camp to relieve himself and found Kira awake when he returned. "Good morning," he greeted. Her smile seemed to encompass her entire face.

"How did you sleep?" she asked, crawling out of her bed.

"Better than anything in the past week. What about you?" He offered his hand to her and helped her up off the ground. "Very good." She leaned up and kissed him. They were both in a good mood and quickly packed up their things. Broderick could see storm clouds heading their way.

They mounted their horses and headed toward Ravendale. The dark clouds seemed to approach the city as they did. "How do we get into the city if it is protected?" he asked Kira as they rode. His eyes flickered between the clouds and the city. "Everything should already be arranged. We should be able to walk right in."

He was surprised it would be so easy. Back in Myrwood she made it seem as though it was near to impossible. This would make rescuing his cousin's wife much easier. They were less than a league from the city when the storm hit. Powerful winds whipped at their clothes and buffeted them, threatening to throw them from their horses. Rain came down in a torrential downpour and soaked them almost immediately. They fought against the wind and urged their mounts onward. It took the better part of an hour with the bad weather to reach the borders of Ravendale.

As they approached the city, Broderick could make out the invisible shield that covered the city. The rainwater rolled right off of it. It was an impressive sight. Kira motioned him to stop before they reached the invisible barrier. "We should be able to ride through," she shouted, trying to be heard over the wind and rain. "We don't need to enter through the front gate. We will enter through the East Gate. Just follow me." He nodded in acknowledgement.

They traveled along the outside of the barrier, only visible because of the rain. A short wall surrounded the outside of the city. With a magical barrier protecting them, they had no need of traditional defenses. When they reached the East Gate, the storm seemed to strengthen considerably.

It was too hard to stay atop the horses and so they dismounted. The wind was blowing so fiercely that Broderick feared he would be swept up into the sky. Kira pointed at the barrier. "You first!" she shouted. He nodded. "What happens if your plans have fallen through?" he asked.

"You'll probably be burned to death."

Broderick lost his courage. She stared at him intently, her white eyes searching him, searing him. He shrugged the fear away. She had allowed him into her bed, so why would she lead him to his death?

He turned to the barrier and held his hand out. He took a step. And another. And another. He could hear a humming sound. Gritting his teeth, he put his hand on the barrier.

Nothing happened. He could feel the invisible force field, but it didn't burn him. He was relieved. Perhaps Kira had only been kidding.

Then he heard a cracking sound. Broderick removed his hand and saw a small crack in the barrier where his hand had been. It began to snake out, forking in different directions and spreading everywhere. His eyes widened as the entire barrier was covered in the small cracks. A glaring yellow light began to burn within the cracks. The humming sounded erratic. The cracking sound got louder.

Suddenly, the barrier exploded. Broderick was thrown to the ground by the force, the air blasted from his lungs. He gasped for air and watched as the barrier disintegrated before his eyes.

He looked hurriedly to Kira to make sure she was all right. She was still standing, her eyes alight with a fire that could not be quenched. She strode past him and entered through the gate. He reached out for her but she didn't even bother to look at him.

She disappeared into the city. Finally after several minutes, with air back in his lungs, he was able to struggle to his feet. His chest burned. He grabbed his sword from the saddle of his horse and tied it to his belt. *Where did she go?*

Worried, he went into the city in search for her, leaving the horses tied up at the wall.

Hatred burned within Kira. She stalked through the streets, searching for the right building. She hadn't seen it in years, so she didn't remember what it looked like. But Skiram had described it to her. She had summoned the demon again after Broderick had fallen asleep. She regretted leaving him behind, but she was determined to do this herself. She didn't want him to know.

Commotion and chaos was erupting in the streets. People were shouting and running about. *They know their shield is gone.* She ignored everyone. Pulling out a piece of parchment, she looked it over quickly. Skiram had given it to her. It was a map of Ravendale. Squares and lines outlined various buildings and streets, detailing every section of the city. She looked up and matched her location to the map. *Almost there.*

The building was nondescript. It didn't stand out or have a sign on the front. Even so, everyone who lived in the city knew what it was: the Church. Kira paused at the main entrance. She didn't doubt that it would be guarded. And the priests would no doubt be in an uproar. She looked at the map again, to where she had marked the secret entrance. She would have to be quick. She walked along the building and found the hidden entrance. Kira slid in quietly and was almost run over by a messenger running past. He offered a hasty apology without slowing his pace and was quickly out of sight. She unsheathed the dagger hid in her boot.

The demon had informed her that it was difficult to navigate the building. It was purposefully designed to be like a maze in the event of an attack, back before the priests created the barrier. She passed an ornately decorated door and heard raised voices. She pressed her ear to the door and listened.

"We don't know how it happened," someone said, a note of fear in their voice.

"What do we do?" another said. She heard many voices all talking at once. Once voice in peculiar caught her attention. "Silence!" The other voices quieted. "We must guard the city from our enemies until we can restore the shield. Station priests at each gate. I have ordered the council to convene immediately. You are all dismissed."

She heard people moving around and expected them to exit so she hid in a corner. When the door didn't open, she moved back to see what she could hear. She could make out the same voice muttering curses. She knew it was him. Kira tried the door. It was locked. It seemed the door was really just for decoration. She had to get in that room.

She slid the blade of the dagger in the crack of the door and gently shifted it from side to side. She felt the blade press against something movable. She smiled as she pushed harder and felt the lock *click*. The door opened slightly. She peered into the room through the crack. Years had passed yet she still recognized him. Now she would have justice.

"Kira?" Broderick touched her arm. She jerked away, startled. She growled at him. "You shouldn't be here!" she hissed. "Why? What's going on?" He was confused. She pointed to the way he they had come in. "Wait for me outside."

Broderick raised his brow questioningly but made no move to obey. "We are here to rescue Octavia. Now who do I need to speak with to free her?"

Kira could hear the sound of more people entering the room. "I don't have time for this!" she yelled. Turning, she flung the door open and rushed in, her dagger glittering in the light of the room. Several men were seated and more were entering the room. She saw him sitting at the head of the table. So that's what he was now.

Her father was head of the warrior-priests.

Chapter 10

"Murderer!" she cried as she rushed him. Nobody moved to intercept her, perhaps too startled to realize what was happening. She jumped onto the table and ran toward Morell, kicking up papers and spilling ink vials. He was rising from his seat as she slammed into him, both of them tumbling to the floor.

She flailed wildly, kicking and punching him until she managed to roll atop him. She pressed her dagger to his throat. "You killed my mother!" Emotions surged and roiled within her. Years of anger were swept away by pain and sadness. That horrible event played back in her mind, and for a moment, she was a child again. Tears flowed freely down her face. But then she remembered. She remembered also how he had burned her eyes for having seen it.

The anger rose up through the waves of pain. "I hate you!" she screeched. "I hate you!" She could hear people moving, probably coming to stop her. She drove the blade into his skin, his blood spurting out onto her hands.

She was jerked off her father's body roughly. A man held her arms behind her while another bound her wrists. She didn't bother to struggle. She had done what she came to do. She had killed him. They escorted her from the council room.

Broderick stood in the doorway, his eyes wide with shock. *What just happened?* He saw two men take Kira from the room. Those few who were in the room were silent, not sure what to do. Broderick slowly made his way over to the man lying on the floor, a puddle of blood quickly forming around him.

He knelt beside the body and looked at the man's face. His expression was set in a mixture of surprise and pain. Broderick didn't know why she had killed him, but whatever the reason, no one deserved to die. He laid his hand on the man's head. After a moment, the cut in his neck began to close. One couldn't even tell that there had been any damage to the flesh.

Morell sat up suddenly and gasped in a deep breath. He looked to Broderick. Their eyes met, and Broderick saw the same look in his eyes as he had seen in the others'.

"That man just healed Morell!" someone said. Broderick looked up to see several men, priests by his guess, staring at him. He looked from the men back to Morell. The look was gone. "I've heard of you," Morell said.

"The blonde haired healer."

—

Broderick had spent several hours with Morell and his council. Many of the men were fearful of what the failing of the barrier meant. Broderick knew the shard was responsible for breaking the magic but remained silent. There was no telling what these people would do if they knew he was at fault.

Morell would not allow Broderick to leave his sight. The warrior-priest gave him a tour of the church building and explained what they did to help the people of the city. The more time Broderick spent in Morell's presence, the more he felt uneasy. There was something about the man that Broderick didn't like. He just wasn't sure what it was.

It seemed that nobody had realized Kira was with him. He wanted to see her, but he didn't think it was worth the risk of asking about her. He had a plethora of questions for her. Instead, he had asked open-ended questions to the priests. Who was she? Why did she attack Morell? No one seemed to know. Broderick suspected that Morell knew more about Kira than he was letting on. He learned that Morell had been named the new leader of the church, due to the fact that another candidate had mysteriously disappeared in the night.

The biggest problem was that he had yet to discover any information as to where his cousin's wife was. The note had said to bring the shard to the city …

What if it's a trap? Broderick shuddered at the thought. But what if it was? What if Octavia's captors meant for him to destroy the barrier? And if that was the case, why? He didn't know and he wasn't sure he wanted to find out. Morell finally left his side to see to some issues that had arose. Broderick was relieved that he would get some time alone until he realized that another priest would keep him company.

Broderick began to suspect that he wasn't so much an honored guest as a prisoner. "I could use some fresh air outside these walls," Broderick remarked to his 'guard'. Justus smiled but didn't seem inclined to grant the request. "May I?"

"I don't think that would be wise," Justus answered. "We have many enemies, and if they find out that our barrier has been destroyed, they would attack us. Within these walls you are safest." Broderick pondered the words. *Many enemies.* He had a sick feeling something ill-fated was going to happen. "Are any of these enemies at the gates?" he asked.

Justus shook his head. "No. I don't believe the news has gotten out of the city." *I don't think you've let the news out of the city,* Broderick thought. "When will Morell be back? I do have some pressing business to get back to."

The priest eye Broderick closely. He lowered his voice. "You don't understand, do you? Morell will not let you leave. He may not even let you live." The last statement was barely above a whisper, but Broderick heard every word. "Why do you say that? You are priests. Why would he kill anyone?"

"I've said too much," Justus answered. He remained silent through Broderick's questions. He decided to try a different tactic. "The girl," Broderick said, "the one who tried to kill Morell … where is she?"

Justus shrugged. "Probably in the dungeon." Broderick was taken aback. "The church has a dungeon? That's a bit disturbing." The priest shook his head. "It's not that kind of dungeon. It's really just a space for holding those violent to our cause until they calm down."

"Until you force them to calm down?"

Justus's look warned him he was crossing the line. "I'm sorry," Broderick said, "I just don't understand why anyone would want to kill a priest unless there was something to warrant it."

Justus seemed to hesitate in responding. Finally, he motioned Broderick to follow him. "Come with me." The priest led him down several passages and out into a garden that was open to the sky, but was still located within the building. Flowers and trees of all colors greeted them. Justus made sure no one was nearby and sat on a stone bench. "You can sit if you like," he said. Broderick declined and remained standing.

"There have been whispers," Justus said, keeping his voice low. His eyes kept darting about the garden. "Whispers that—if true—make Morell a very dangerous man." Broderick listened intently. "There are some who say that he is not a man of faith at all, that he seeks only to rule the city."

"Isn't there a separation of the affairs of faith and of politics?"

"There is supposed to be. But everyone knows the church is really running Ravendale. It's not as bad as it sounds. The people are safer in our hands than in the hands of a tyrannical man without faith."

Broderick shrugged. It wasn't important to him whether that was true or not. "Some think this is true. Things have happened that seem like divine intervention on Morell's behalf, but many think otherwise. They think he is strong arming anyone who disagrees with him. And there are some who think he has them … disposed of."

"Killed?"

Justus nodded. "I am among the latter. I wasn't until recently. He made a comment the day before the council was to choose between him and Rainor, the other candidate. He claimed he was joking, but then mysteriously Rainor disappears in the night and there is no trace of him. Morell is claiming it is the hand of God showing that he was meant to be leader."

"You don't believe him?" Broderick asked. Justus shook his head.

"I want to believe him, but I cannot. My conscious will not allow me to. If a man were going to up and leave, he would have taken some of his belongings, at least. Everything he owned was still in his home. It's too suspicious for me."

"That's understandable. If these things are true, how did he get elected as leader?"

Justus sighed. "There is no proof to all these rumors. And the council is too afraid to stand against him now that Rainor has gone missing."

"What about Kir—the girl who tried to kill him?"

Justus didn't seem to notice the slip up. He scratched his chin. "I'm not sure. If any of these rumors are true, there is bound to be someone who wants him dead. I know he was married when he first entered the church, but I don't know that he had any children. There's no telling truth from lie with him, it seems."

"Has anyone questioned the girl? Maybe she could give some answers to these questions, and you would have your proof." Broderick didn't care about the politics of the church, he just wanted to free Kira and find Octavia. "Are there any other prisoners with her?"

Justus shook his head. "She's the only one. We haven't had to lock anyone in there in years. As to questioning her … I don't know if that would be wise. Even if she had information, how would it look trying to use her word against him when she tried to kill him?" Broderick conceded the point. "I would like to talk to her," he said. Justus hesitated but finally agreed to let him. "I know it may not do anything to expose Morell, but perhaps we can learn how she navigated her way to the council room," the priest said. "It is a tightly kept secret. Perhaps she isn't the only one that wants him dead."

The dungeon wasn't really a dungeon at all. It was simply decorated. A bowl of fruit rested in the center of a round table. A few padded chairs surrounded the table, and Kira sat on one of them. A guard was posted at the doorway of the room. Justus dismissed him and took up his post to keep watch so that Broderick could talk to her.

Her eyes lit up with excitement when she saw him, but he motioned her to be quiet. *We don't know each other,* he mouthed to her. She nodded. He was completely direct with his questions. Finally, he asked the one that he really wanted to know.

"Why did you try to kill Morell?"

She bit her lip. She looked pleadingly at him, silently begging him not to make her answer. He remained stoic. She cast her eyes down. "He is my father," she said softly. "When I was a child, he killed my mother. I saw him do it," she said brokenly. "He … he burned my eyes with a piece of hot steel."

The answer left Broderick wordless. "He deserved to be brought to justice. I made a deal with a demon to find my way to him. His death has been long in coming."

Broderick knelt before her. "He's not dead," he said. Confusion contorted her face. "I cut his throat. I saw him die."

He didn't know how to phrase it. He didn't want to tell her. She would be angry with him. "You didn't," she breathed. He lowered his head. "I didn't know," he answered. "He is alive."

Her breathing quickened. She scowled at him. "Get away from me," she growled. "Leave!" Broderick rose to his feet but tried to calm her. "I have to find Octavia," he said. "I need your help."

"You stole my justice," she spat. "Your cousin's wife isn't here. She never was. I planted that note. I don't know who took her. I *used you* to bring down the barrier so that I could kill my father." The viciousness in her voice stung him profoundly. Tears welled up in his eyes. "I'm sorry," he said again.

"Leave me," she reiterated. He turned away and walked slowly to where Justus stood. He didn't pronounce judgment or say anything at all. The priest could tell there was much more to their argument than he could understand. A loud trumpet sounded. Justus seemed uneasy. "What is that?" Broderick asked.

"I'm not sure," Justus answered. Another priest came running. "Goblins!" he screamed. "Goblins are attacking the city!"

Chapter 11

Justus led Broderick out of the building, pointing toward the nearest city gate. "If you hurry, you should be out of the city before the goblins reach this point. And don't worry about the girl," the priest added, seeing the troubled look on Broderick's face. "I will make sure she is safe."

Broderick hesitated. He thought maybe he could convince her to come with him, but her angry words echoed in his mind. He shook Justus's hand and left, running through the empty streets. Apparently the people took to hiding in their homes while the priests defended the city. He reached the gate without incident. His sword had been taken after he had brought Morell back to life, but Justus had given it back to him before showing him the way out.

The main problem he faced now was that his horse was on the other side of the city. He thought it unlikely he could reach it without being attacked, and so he continued on foot. He reached the road that led east and stopped. Looking back, he could see plumes of smoke rising from the city. Could it be the same goblins that attacked the farm? And if they were, why were they still following him? Broderick hoped that nobody would be hurt. He looked away from Ravendale and considered his options. He had no idea where his cousin's wife was.

The betrayal he felt stung him deeply. How could Kira have lied to him? He sighed. He could continue east but he had no idea where he would go. He also considered turning back and going home. How would he explain to his cousin that he gave up the search? He couldn't bring himself to do that. As he decided to head east, he heard the sound of an approaching horse. Broderick looked toward the sound and saw a man clothed in black and hooded, riding a black horse. The rider thundered toward him. Broderick stared at the figure.

Something about the rider seemed familiar. As the man and his mount past him on the road, the figure stared right back at Broderick. After they had passed, the man turned his head back and continued at the quick pace. Then it hit him. Back at his cousin's estate, when he was walking the fields, he thought he saw a man in black near the woods. It had to be the same person.

Broderick took off running after the horse. Logically he knew he wouldn't be able to catch up to them. Even if the horse tired out soon, they were already out of his sight. But now he had a plan. It couldn't have been a coincidence that the man in black had been sneaking around the estate the same night Octavia had been captured. Now he just had to catch up to the man and trail him.

—

Kira sat sullenly in her chair. She refused to believe she had come this far and failed. Well, she hadn't failed. Broderick had failed her. Ration told her to forgive him. He didn't know why she had killed her father. That was her fault. Instead of telling him the truth earlier, she had used him as an unwitting pawn in her scheme to bring down the barrier. And now the one thing she had gained was lost, all because of her stubbornness.

And on top of everything else, goblins were attacking the city. She could probably escape right now if she wanted to. But what was the point? Her father was still alive, and … wait. If she killed him once, she could do it again. And this time, her emotions wouldn't hinder her. She glanced furtively into the hall. She didn't see anyone. She knew her dagger was in the wooden chest across from her. She had seen Justus retrieve Broderick's sword from it and assumed her own weapon must be there.

She stood up and walked over to the chest. It was still open. Justus had led Broderick out in a hurry and had probably forgotten. She looked inside. It was empty. She bit her lip in frustration. Kira froze as she felt strong hands grab her from behind and felt the cold metal of a blade pressed on her neck.

"Well," her father said, "it looks like it's just the two of us."

She shuddered in his grasp. "Just kill me and get it over with," she spat angrily. Morell laughed. "And why would I want to do that? You are much more valuable to me alive. For now, at least."

Kira was confused. "What do you want?" she demanded, struggling to get out of his grasp. He was still so strong despite being so much older and she failed to do anything other than nick her flesh on the blade. She could feel blood drip down her neck. She swallowed hard and decided that struggling was useless. "What do you want from me?" she asked again, her tone reflecting the defeat she felt in her spirit.

"I knew you would come to see it my way," Morell said. "It is not what I want from you, but what I want from your friend. He carries something very powerful, of that I am sure. I want it."

Kira feigned ignorance. "Friend? I have no friends. If you are talking about the man here earlier, the one who questioned me, I don't know him."

Morell's grip on her tightened. "Don't play coy with me," he whispered dangerously. "I'm not as gullible as you think. The chances of a man who can bring back the dead—and I was dead—traveling with the 'Necromancer' is nothing short of miraculous, wouldn't you say?" He pressed the dagger, *her* dagger, against her neck harder. "Want to try again?"

She ground her teeth. He had defeated her again. "His name is Broderick, and he is a healer. I don't know much more than that. We traveled here together for different purposes. And I'm not the Necromancer."

"I don't believe that. There hasn't been a real healer since the days of the priest Tymothy. I've heard it on good authority something fell from the sky, and not long after word of a healer starts spreading through the towns. And I know you are the Necromancer. All it took was a little investigation after hearing of a wizard who had white eyes. I have to say I am impressed. I thought I blinded you, and yet here you are. And you even managed to kill me."

He had actually blinded her. Mostly, anyway. She could only make out blurred shapes then. She had run away and eventually learned the dark craft she practiced from an old crone of a woman. The demon Skiram had restored her sight, if not her irises. She would not give Morell anymore power over her than he already had, however. Kira didn't want him to know anything else about her.

"So what does this have to do with me?"

Morell turned her around to face him but kept the blade ready to kill her if he needed. "I want you to get whatever he has and bring it to me." Now it was Kira's turn to laugh. "I don't even know where he is. And if I did, there is no way I would bring you anything." She spat on the ground.

"You will do it, or I will. Trust me when I say that you don't want me to fetch him. You'd never see him again."

Her heart sunk at the threat. She knew her father well enough to know he would carry it out. If she went, he would live. She lowered her head in resignation. "I'll do it," she said softly. Morell grinned wickedly.

Chapter 12

Ferrin paced back and forth across the room, his steps dragging as slow as the time passed. He was impatiently waiting for word from his apprentices. A knock at the door turned his attention from his dark thoughts. "Enter," he commanded.

The door opened on silent hinges and he was pleased to see that it was Vius. The young man entered and shut the door behind him. Ferrin liked Vius. As much as he could like another human being, anyway. He was in his twenties, young and full of life. His hair was cut short and the color of leaves after all life has left them. Were his powers not so weakened, Ferrin would have simply possessed one of his apprentices like he did ages ago.

"Have you found it?"

Vius paused and thought how to best phrase the bad news. Ferrin was known for his angry outbursts. "We did find it," he answered. Ferrin nodded approvingly. "Let me have it," he said. Vius shifted uneasily. "We do not have it in our possession," he informed his master. He flinched involuntarily, expecting a verbal lashing. When it did not come, he looked at Ferrin, confused.

"Where is it?" Ferrin asked. Vius cleared his throat. "A man has it. He was staying at a house in Myrwood. We attempted to steal it from him in the night, but he wasn't at the house. So we took a woman who lived there as ransom."

Ferrin's eyes glittered in the candlelight of the room. "Has he come forth to trade it for the woman?" Vius shook his head. "Why not?"

Vius opened his mouth to speak, then closed it. He was not about to take the wrath of their master because his fellow apprentice had not done his task. "I think it is because the man doesn't know where to find us."

Ferrin laid his forehead in his left hand. "And why would that be, exactly?" Vius felt his skin begin to crawl under his master's scrutinizing gaze. He also felt power begin to pool around Ferrin, the air thrumming with energy. "I instructed the mute one to leave a note. It seems … he forgot."

Ferrin nodded. That one had been a nuisance for a long time now. Perhaps it was time to teach a lesson on failure. "The man who has it is obviously a wizard. When he comes for the girl, we must crush him without mercy."

"The man is not a wizard."

Ferrin's brow creased upward in disbelief. "Then why do we not have it in our possession?" His level of frustration was beginning to boil over into anger.

"The object you seek seems to have given him powers. Myrwood was blazing with rumors of a man who had brought back the dead and healed the sick. When we realized the man was performing these miracles because of what he found, it was too late. We would not have been able to take it by force with him surrounded by the crowds of people who flock to see him.

"So we attempted to steal it under cover of night. There was one who came to the man known as the Necromancer. It appears she is helping him to rescue the woman." Ferrin nodded at the mention of the Necromancer. He had heard of her, though she posed little threat to him. Still, why would she not take the shard for herself? The thought plagued his mind. "What then are you doing here if you have not retrieved the shard yet?"

Vius hoped this news would be good enough to sate his master's wrath. "I came because I have other news. The magical shield over Ravendale has fallen."

Were he not so old, Ferrin might have leapt about in excitement. The news invigorated him. "This is good news. You did well in returning to tell me. How did it fall? Have the warrior-priests lost their powers?"

Vius shook his head. "From what I could gather, someone destroyed it." Ferrin was surprised to hear that. He was confident there was no wizard stronger than he, and his attempt to bring down the shield ended horribly. "Who was it? It couldn't have been Nidrea. She isn't strong enough."

"No, it was not Nidrea. A priest offered me some interesting information for his life. It seems a man who healed their dead master came into town around the same time the barrier came down. It seems this shard's powers are considerable, to say the least."

Interesting, thought Ferrin. With power like that, he could do much more than heal his body. *And this man is parading around healing people. What a waste.* "Is this man still in Ravendale?"

"I don't believe so. The city was attacked by a large force of goblins. As I left the city, I passed a man on the road. It seemed odd to me that he was traveling from the direction of the city and had no signs of having been fighting. I think he might be the man we are looking for."

Ferrin thought about everything his apprentice told him. "When was this?"

"Four days ago," Vius answered. "Though I was on horseback and he was on foot. There's no telling where he might be now. Also, the Necromancer wasn't with him."

"Interesting," muttered Ferrin. Was it possible that he killed the white eyed witch? He didn't know. Yet if the shard could bring down the barrier, perhaps the man had killed the Necromancer as well. "Seek this man out and bring him to me. Do not come back until you have him."

Vius bowed in obedience. He turned to leave but paused in the doorway. "What of the woman?" he asked.

"Kill her," Ferrin said nonchalantly.

—

"Take her down to the dungeon and do it," Vius instructed. Liam bowed his head in submission and took Octavia by the arm and led her down to the lower part of the castle. As he guided her through the confusing maze of corridors, he considered how she had ceased her fighting. Perhaps she had given up hope. Liam frowned. This wasn't what he had signed up for. Vius had recruited him, lured him into his apprenticeship with promises of power and wealth.

Liam had come to realize the cost of such power too late. His first mistake had cost him his voice. He remembered vividly how harshly Ferrin had disciplined him. And then he had commanded Vius to permanently silence him. His free hand involuntarily went to his neck. He pushed the thoughts to the back of his mind as they reached the main chamber of the dungeon. Liam forced Octavia down to her knees and pushed her head onto a square-shaped flat surface. He grabbed an ax that hung from the wall and ran his finger along the blade.

It sliced right through his skin. A small drop of blood seeped out from the cut. He nodded his head in satisfaction. He hefted the ax up with both hands and looked down at her. All of the fight may have gone from her, but she stared back at him unwaveringly. Her eyes said what she couldn't. They pleaded with him to spare her.

Liam sighed and lowered the ax. Who was he kidding? He was no murderer. He placed the ax back on the wall and helped Octavia up. He tried to think of what he could do with her. He couldn't just set her free to wander the frozen lands of Eurn alone. He led her to one of the cells in the darker area of the dungeon. He made sure she had some food and enough water and locked her in the cell. He knew he couldn't keep her there indefinitely, but he couldn't kill her either. Liam sighed again and headed back to the upper chambers, heavily burdened.

Chapter 13

Broderick had spent the last two days traveling from town to town seeking information on the black clothed man. Most everyone he talked to hadn't seen anyone that matched his description. Broderick was starting to wonder if he had gone the wrong direction when he reached a small village and received the same answers to his questions.

An old man in one of the taverns, however, piqued his interest. He had a small gathering of people around him and at first Broderick thought the old man was telling a story. When he walked by, he heard some of what was being said.

"I was afraid for my life. He looked normal enough, but there was something about him that radiated evil. He wore all black, and his horse was black as well. I saw him do something odd with his hands and then there was a bright flash of light. He was a wizard, I've no doubt."

Broderick had waited until the small crowd dispersed, bored with the old man's story. Then he had made his way over to the man's table and asked to join him. The old man, eager for more attention, obliged him.

"The story you just told everyone. Is it true?" The old man scowled at him. "You think I'm lying, do you?" He puffed his chest out indignantly. Broderick had stifled his laughter at the man's attempt of bravado. *He couldn't be younger than seventy years,* Broderick had mused. "No, no. I don't think you are lying. What I meant was, are all the details true? You didn't exaggerate any of them?"

The old man took a sip from his brass tankard and shook his head. "I'm too old to be telling fanciful tales, my boy. What would be the point? Besides, I've seen much more interesting things than that in my long life. I was a child during the demon invasion, you know?"

Broderick doubted that, but he humored the man to get some answers. "This man that you saw. He wore all black, you said?" The man nodded and took another drink of his brew. "That he was. Could have been leather, but from the way it swayed in the wind, I'd say it was more likely made of cloth. He had a hood, too, but it fell off his head and that's how I saw he was an ordinary man. Except for the magic, of course."

"Of course," Broderick agreed absently. "Which way was he traveling?" The old man scratched the side of his head and squinted his eyes. "North," he finally answered. He had attempted to explain how he knew it was north, where he was standing as he watched the man ride away, and other trivial details. He had thanked the man and went on his way.

Now he stood at the edge of town and stared at the road that forked. One way to the east, and the other to the north. What if the old man was wrong? What if the black clothed rider went east instead of north? He sighed. If he found nothing to the north, then he would come back and go east. He had bought a horse two towns back and had sped up his search tremendously. That and his feet had gotten blistered from walking such long distances.

He mounted his horse and headed north. The hours burned away as he rode on. The road was well worn, but he didn't see any more towns. Eventually he stopped next to a small stream to water his horse and rest. It was mid-afternoon and he was beginning to wonder if he would find a comfortable place to rest. After his mount had drank its fill, he continued his trek. Several hours later he still hadn't found another town. The air had cooled tremendously and Broderick thought he could see snow in the distance. He found a spot beneath a small copse of trees that seemed the best place to rest.

After tethering his horse to one of the branches, he laid out his blanket and stared up into the sky. It was quiet and peaceful. It reminded him of his home on the lake. He got homesick and tried to turn his thoughts to other things. He wondered how Derrick was doing without his wife. *Probably not very well,* Broderick thought.

The sound of twigs breaking caused him to sit up. His horse nickered softly but didn't seem alarmed. Broderick got up and unsheathed his sword. There was no telling what sort of animals roamed the wilds here. He moved cautiously in the direction he had heard the sound. There were few clouds in the sky and the moon was bright, giving him plenty of light by which to see. A hundred feet or so away he spotted a deer. It was brown and speckled with white splotches. It raised its ears in alarm as it sniffed at the air, then turned and darted away into the trees.

"Just a deer," Broderick said to himself, thankful it wasn't something aggressive. A splitting pain erupted in the back of his head and he crumbled to the ground in a heap. His vision blurred and was starting to go dark. He heard voices but he couldn't make out what they were saying. Before blackness took him, he felt as though he were flying.

—

Broderick awoke to find his wrists chained to a wall above his head. He groaned aloud as he felt his head pounding. *Where am I?* His grogginess slowly faded and he began to study his surroundings. He was in a small cell. The chains that manacled his wrists were attached to iron rings that had been drilled into the stone wall behind him. He was freezing and his throat was parched.

He attempted to stand and found it difficult to do so. Using the chains as leverage, he managed to get to his feet. The chains were shorter than he would have liked and he couldn't reach the gate to his cell. It probably wouldn't have done any good anyway, as he assumed it was locked.

"Hey!" he called out. "Let me out of here!" His words echoed off the stone walls around him and seemed not to reach anyone. Rats scurried about on the floor. He didn't know where he was or what had happened. Apparently from the way his head was pounding he had taken a pretty strong blow. He had no way of knowing how much time had passed and slumped back down the wall. He was starting to doze off when he heard the sound of boots thumping down the hall in front of his cell.

There was hardly any light, but he could see the outline of the black clothed man he had been trying to trail. "Who are you?" he demanded. There was no answer. Broderick heard the jingling of keys as the man unlocked the gate and stepped inside. It was too dark to make out any of the figure's details. The man grabbed Broderick's wrists and unlocked the manacles. Then he roughly lifted him up and pushed him out of the cell. All of his questions and demands were met with silence. The man guided him through the dim corridors into a chamber that reminded Broderick of a tavern.

Various multi-colored tapestries hung from the walls depicting an array of scenes. An enormous table rested in the center of the room, covered with a multitude of papers. The man pushed him into one of the chairs at the table and motioned for him to stay put then disappeared through one of the doors. In the light, he realized this was not the same man he had been tracking.

Broderick curiously looked over the papers on the table. The writing was nothing he had ever seen before. Various runes and symbols were drawn all over the papers. There was one word that he could make out. The same word that was etched into the blade his cousin had given him: Sorandra.

He considered the coincidence for a moment before he heard the door swing open. He was greeted by an old man, much older than the one he met at the village. His head was devoid of any hair at all, and his face was creased with many wrinkles. The man shuffled slowly over to the table, resting his weight on a staff. The man was dressed similarly to the mute man, though this man's clothes were of much better quality. They were flowing black robes trimmed in silver. The old man sat down and studied Broderick in silence for long moments.

He made a motion with his hand and the other man brought a sword to him. The old man unsheathed it and laid it across the table. Broderick saw it was his own sword. "Do you know the history of this blade?" the old man asked. His voice was low and cracked with age. Broderick didn't answer. *Why should I? They've imprisoned me.*

Under the old man's harsh gaze, however, Broderick's resolve melted. "No. It was a gift from my cousin. Who are you? And why am I here?" In the silence, Broderick could hear the old man wheezing.

The old man ran his fingers along the blade of the sword, feeling every rune etched on its surface. "My name is Ferrin. And you are here because you have something I want. We will have time for your questions later. This sword," Ferrin nodded at it, "is a powerful relic from an ancient time. This blade was crafted in the Starforge Mountains by a warrior-mage of great renown. It was to serve a single purpose: to destroy evil. The enchantments on it protect the wielder from many things. How did your cousin come across it, I wonder?"

Broderick decided that stubbornness would likely get him nowhere. "I don't know. He only said it was in his family for a long time." Ferrin stared at him intently. "That may be true," he said, more to himself than to Broderick. The silence resumed. Broderick grew frustrated. "What is it that I have that would make you violently attack me?" he said angrily.

"There is no need to get upset," Ferrin said. "Just ask my apprentice there." He pointed toward the other man. Broderick looked to him, and Liam pulled the collar of his robe down to reveal a large scar across his throat. Broderick shuddered at the sight and looked back at the old man. "Bad things happen when people get upset." Ferrin smiled maliciously.

"There is something you found, something small that fell from the sky. I want it." Ferrin leaned forward and stretched out his hand. Broderick eyed Ferrin's hand distrustfully. "Why would I give it to you?" he questioned.

"To keep from dying," Ferrin answered curtly. "I could boil the flesh off your body with a single word if I so desired. I can torment you in ways that will leave you wishing for death, yet it will not come." Broderick had no doubts that Ferrin could—and would—commit such atrocities against him.

"Why didn't you just take it from me while I was unconscious? Wouldn't that have saved you the headache of waiting for me to wake up? And then you could have killed me or dumped me somewhere. Why all this?" Broderick motioned his hand to encompass the room.

"That wouldn't be any fun," Ferrin replied. "I want to see how the shard works," he added. He rose from his chair and ordered his apprentice to come near. Liam knelt down before Ferrin. The old man placed his hand on the apprentice's head and begin to whisper words that gave Broderick chills. The mute man opened his mouth in a silent cry of pain and fell to the floor. He squirmed on the ground, blood spilling out of his eyes.

Broderick stared, horrified. "What are you doing to him?" he cried out. Ferrin watched it all with an emotionless detachment that bewildered Broderick. After some more thrashing about, the man lay still in his own blood. Ferrin turned his fiery gaze on Broderick. "Touch him," he commanded. Broderick's mind screamed at him to stay put, that the mute man was better off dead than serving this vile creature of a man.

Yet his body betrayed him and he watched his own hand reach out and touch the dead man. As with the others, a few moments passed and then the man opened his eyes. He had the same look as the others as well. The man coughed a few times and a look of confusion crossed over his face. He got to his feet and looked at Ferrin. "I … I was … dead." The words came out hesitantly, as though he didn't know how to speak.

Ferrin was impressed. Not only had the shard brought his apprentice back to life, it healed the damage to his vocal chords. This was powerful magic indeed. "Give me the shard," he said, excitement tingling throughout his old bones. Broderick took a step back away from him. Ferrin scowled at him and shuffled toward him.

Suddenly the room shook violently. Trails of dust fell from between the stones in the ceiling. All three of them looked about, trying to figure out what just happened. And then the room shook again, stronger this time. Ferrin got a wild look in his eyes and fled the room as quickly as his legs would allow him. The man who had been mute looked at Broderick, then followed his master.

Broderick got up and grabbed his sword off the table. He didn't know what was going on, but it was the perfect distraction to stage an escape. He left the chamber through the same door as Ferrin. A long corridor ended at two large wooden doors. He ran to the doors and pressed his ear to the wood to see what he could hear.

There was no sound. He pulled on the door but it didn't budge. *How did the old man open it?* he wondered. He sheathed the sword and tied it to his belt. Wrapping both hands around the handle, he heaved with all his might. The door begrudgingly creaked opened slowly. The door was thick and heavy and Broderick's muscles bulged under the strain. He finally got it open enough to slide through the breach.

A large open courtyard spread out before him. He had never seen anything so massive. He saw Ferrin and two other men standing on the battlements. Now was his chance. He saw a door on the right wall and ran for it. Out of the shadows a third man stepped out to meet him. Broderick halted and drew his sword. "Move out of my way and I won't cut you down," he threatened. The man didn't seem impressed. The man was wearing the same clothes as the others.

Vius wasn't going to let the man escape with the shard. He blocked the way with his body, prepared to stop him. He lifted his hand and unleashed a blast of flames from his hand. The heat drove Broderick back a few steps, but the flames died as they neared him. The wizard looked perplexed at this and cast the fire forth again.

Again, the flames died as they approached him. Vius snarled and stalked toward him. Broderick raised the sword menacingly. Vius grabbed the blade in his hand and yanked it from Broderick's grasp. The metal bit into his flesh but he ignored the pain and flung the blade across the courtyard. Vius slugged Broderick in his jaw, knocking him down. Blood dripped from Vius's palm.

Broderick was dazed and didn't fight when Vius jerked him up and dragged him to the stairs that led up to the battlements where Ferrin stood. Broderick reluctantly climbed the stairs and looked out over the wall. A sizeable army greeted him. And in the front was the unmistakable form of his cousin. And next to him was Kira.

"Release my cousin!" Derrick demanded loudly. Ferrin laughed. "Do you honestly think your pathetic weapons serve you here?"

Derrick and Kira parted to reveal an older woman, wearing robes of a similar style as those Ferrin wore. "Nidrea," Ferrin spat. "You would betray me?" he asked the sorceress. "It pays well," she replied with a shrug. "Now release him. Or I will tear apart your castle stone by stone."

"I'll let you choose," Ferrin called back. "You can have this one, or the woman." Derrick looked to Nidrea and then back to Ferrin. "What woman?"

"Your wife," Ferrin replied.

Chapter 14

"I'm sorry, Broderick," Derrick said. Emotions erupted across his face. "I choose my wife."

"Don't worry about me!" Broderick shouted to his cousin. Ferrin motioned to Liam. "Bring her body," he instructed. Broderick was about to say something when Vius punched him in the mouth, then wrapped his arm around Broderick's neck and jerked him away from the wall. Broderick struggled against him, but Vius was stronger.

Liam left quickly, running down the stairs and into the castle. How was he going to explain the woman still being alive? Fear gripped him as he thought about the horrible pain Ferrin would inflict upon him. He navigated through the castle and down to the dungeon, pausing outside the cell he had locked the woman in. He considered what to do. He doubted that Ferrin would overlook this discretion. Liam knew he was expendable to Ferrin.

He kicked the cell door in frustration, startling the woman. "I'm sorry," he said haltingly. Though his voice had returned, he had trouble forming the words after spending so long in silence. What was he going to do? He couldn't bring her up there alive. He couldn't return without a body. And he certainly couldn't simply not return.

Unless.

Liam smiled as he considered that very course of action. He could sneak the woman out one of the side entrances and leave also. Ferrin would try to hunt him down, he knew. But he considered it worth the risk. He had already died, what could be worse?

"Lady," he said as he unlocked the cell. "I hope you feel up to running." Octavia looked at him questioningly. "We're going to escape this place," he informed her. "Stay close, and whatever happens, run as fast as you can when we get outside the walls."

Liam helped her to her feet and led her out of the cell. "Are you ready?" he asked her. She nodded her head resolutely. "I am."

—

Ferrin scowled at Vius. "Where is he? He is taking too long." Vius shrugged, thinking the same thing himself. "I'll get him."

"No," Ferrin interrupted. "I need you to keep *him*—" he pointed to Broderick—"subdued. Do not let him move."

"What's taking so long, Ferrin? I should hope you are not foolish enough to play games with me," Nidrea said accusingly. She folded her arms across her chest. Ferrin growled under his breath. He raised his hand and quickly chanted several words. The air around him crackled and a bolt of lightning flung forth from his hand, arcing dangerously through the air before striking Nidrea to the ground. Derrick and Kira flung themselves out of the way and avoided the worst, but they were both disoriented.

Nidrea got up from the ground, her clothes singed and smoking. "So this is what you resort to?" she screamed at him. "Attacking a fellow sorcerer?" She raised her arms and traced symbols into the air, weaving her fingers in intricate patterns. The ground began to shake violently, causing the soldiers to cry out. Nidrea ignored them and kept the spell going. The stone wall of the castle began to shake as well. Some of the stones began to shake free of the wall, crashing to the ground with thunderous sounds.

Ferrin wrapped his hands around his staff and slammed the butt of it down. "Be still," he commanded. Nidrea's spell suddenly failed and the ground stopped heaving. The surprise was evident on her face. Ferrin smirked at her, then pointed his staff toward her and began to chant again, calling the power of the air to his aid. Dark clouds began to swirl above them. The soldiers began to flee in terror. Derrick shouted for them to stop, but they didn't listen. A vicious wind picked up, whipping snow and ice around violently. "*Duun igar sy namanu!*" Ferrin shouted.

A vortex of flames descended from the clouds. Nidrea knelt down and summoned a shield to protect her. A pale blue light flared up around her, protecting her from the heat and the fire. Ferrin repeated the phrase two more times, causing two more identical vortexes of flame to join the first. The old wizard cackled madly. His eyes were bloodshot and sweat gathered on his brow. He began to move his staff in a circle, and as he did so, the three twisters of fire began to spin around Nidrea.

Ferrin decided in that moment that he had allowed her to thwart his will long enough. He dropped his staff and put his hands together, rubbing them together faster and faster. The three twisters began to spin around Nidrea rapidly, slowly coalescing until it was a solid spherical wall of intense flames. He watched the whirlwind of flames, spiraling meters high, spinning round and round. *It was like a scene from Hell*, Ferrin thought. He held his hands up and blew into them. The flames intensified for a moment and then went out, leaving the charred remains of Nidrea in its wake.

Vius gaped at the display of power, unknowingly loosening his hold on Broderick. Vius grunted as Broderick elbowed him in the stomach, blasting the breath from him. He broke free of Vius's hold, turned, and kicked him off the wall. The apprentice flailed wildly as he fell backward, landing with a dull thud in the courtyard. Broderick turned his attention to Ferrin. He sprinted toward the old man, intending to tackle him to the ground.

Quicker than Broderick thought possible, Ferrin swept up his staff and pointed it at Broderick. He chanted off another spell and using his staff, stopped Broderick's momentum with a suddenness that made Broderick gasp.

Ferrin held him in place and shuffled slowly over to him. "I've had enough fun," he said. The old wizard snatched the leather pouch that contained the shard from Broderick's belt and then flung Broderick off the wall with a jerk of his staff.

Broderick flew through the air and landed roughly on the ground, skidding to a stop. He could feel his skin burning and cried out in pain. Darkness threatened to overwhelm him, but he forced himself to stay conscious. He crawled toward the gate he attempted to escape from earlier. Then he saw Octavia and Liam slinking in the shadows, heading in the same direction. He got up and tried to run, but instead stumbled along. The pain in his legs was almost unbearable. He looked back fearfully, thinking Ferrin would be there to strike him down. Ferrin's attention was consumed by the shard. Broderick could see the glint of the stone in the old wizard's hand.

Broderick lamented its loss, but he knew life would be easier without it. He looked to where Vius had fallen and saw he still lay there, unmoving. He looked back to the gate to see Octavia and Liam disappear through it. He pushed himself harder and managed to lurch through the gate. He was out of the castle, but still far from freedom. He reached Derrick and Kira shortly after Octavia did. Liam was nowhere to be seen.

He tripped and fell, panting heavily. Kira helped him up. They stared into each other's eyes in silence. Kira lowered her head. "I'm sorry," she said softly. "You were right. You didn't know what Morell did. I can't lose you," she said brokenly. Broderick touched her face and smiled. "I forgive you. We can talk about this later, we have to get out of here."

"Can you make it?" Derrick asked, concerned. Broderick nodded. "We have to hurry. I fear Ferrin will be quick behind us." Kira nodded in agreement. "Now hurry!" Derrick led them away from the castle. Broderick leaned on Kira for support and followed his cousin.

After nearly an hour, they reached a massive campsite. The small contingent of men that Derrick had hired had retreated back to it. The commander of the force greeted them sheepishly as they approached. "My apologies," he said with a bow. "My men are not accustomed to fighting against magic. I will refund everything you paid us."

"It seems loyalty is cheap these days," Derrick replied. The commander lowered his head in disgrace. "Pack up camp and let's get out of here," Derrick ordered. The commander shook his head. "We shouldn't travel at night. There's no telling what we will come against in this place. And it's too cold to travel. Let us rest and we can leave first thing in the morning."

Derrick didn't argue, he was too tired to. He merely nodded. The commander left and Derrick turned to the three of them. "I thought I'd never see you again," he said to Octavia. He kissed her passionately and held her close for long moments. He hesitantly released his wife. She was sobbing. "How is Claire?" she asked after she had gathered control of herself.

"She is fine," he assured her. Then he embraced Broderick. "Cousin, I thought you were dead. When you didn't return, I feared the worst. I hired this band of mercenaries and searched the countryside. I found the Necromancer after the soldiers slaughtered a horde of goblins that was attacking Ravendale. She led us to Nidrea," his expression darkened, "who in turn led us to that castle. It pains me that she died so horribly."

"She knew what she was up against," Kira said. "Ferrin is a powerful wizard. And now that he knows you have the shard, there is no telling what he will do to get it."

"Let's not worry about that right now," Broderick said. "If I don't get off my legs, I may pass out." Kira helped Broderick over to one of the many fires the soldiers had lit for warmth. They nestled next to each other. Kira stroked her fingers through his hair and stared at him. "I feared we would not reach you in time," she whispered.

"But you did," he replied. They sat in silence for a long while. Broderick was exhausted but he could not fall asleep. Eventually the fire began to burn low. "I'll put some more wood in it," Broderick said. He struggled to get up. Kira pushed him down. "You rest. I'll get it." She got up and wandered over to a large pile of logs the soldiers had cut and returned with a few of them. She tossed them into the embers and returned to Broderick's side.

She helped him sit up and they sat staring into the flames. The fire sputtered suddenly, as if something were thrown into it. The flames wavered, convulsed, and then split down the middle. Kira saw the familiar face of Skiram in the fire. She eyed the demon distrustfully. "I did not summon you," she said. Broderick trembled. "What is that?" he asked tremulously.

"He is a demon," she answered, not taking her eyes off the foul creature. Skiram's face split into a grin and the demon laughed. "You share your bed with him, but you don't share your life?" Skiram taunted. Kira growled in anger. "Leave Skiram, or I will vanquish you right now!"

Skiram's face grew serious. "I have come to name my sacrifice, foolish woman. In nine months time, I will come to you again and you will honor our deal." Kira's face scrunched up in confusion. "Nine months? What are you talking about? Take your sacrifice now and be done with our deal. I want nothing more to do with you," she spat.

Skiram laughed again. "I would take my sacrifice now, but it is not ready. It must yet grow within you." Broderick clenched Kira's hand in his, not understanding any of it. Realization slowly dawned on Kira.

"No," she snarled. "No! I will not honor our deal!"

"What is happening?" Broderick asked. He looked from Kira to the demon. Skiram seemed to enjoy the torment that was evident on Kira's face. "Don't you know?" the demon asked. "That's right … you don't. The Necromancer and I made a deal. The knowledge of the secret entrance into the church in Ravendale for a sacrifice of my choosing."

"What are you asking of her? I will fulfill the deal," Broderick said. Skiram's face contorted oddly as the demon laughed a third time. "I am afraid you aren't able to," Skiram said. "The sacrifice is hers alone to give. You are bound to honor our deal. There is no way to break it, as you well know. I demand the life of the child growing within you," Skiram said with finality. The flames shot up into the air and then faded from sight, leaving the fire as if nothing had happened.

"Child?" Broderick repeated. He looked dazedly at Kira. "Yes," she said, staring sadly into the fire. Her hand moved to her stomach.

"Our child."

Chapter 15

Ferrin stood in his personal chambers, staring intently at the shard. He could feel the power of the stone thrumming in his hand. Vius stood nearby, bruised and bloody. Ferrin felt different somehow. He hadn't used the magic yet, but he felt it flowing through him. His steps were lighter, his muscles didn't ache from age.

He looked to Vius. His strongest apprentice had almost died. Jole hadn't returned from his task, and Liam had abandoned them. Ferrin didn't care about that. He had the shard. "Are you in pain?" he asked. Vius didn't know how to respond. If he said yes, Ferrin would see it as weakness. If he said no, Ferrin would call him a liar. He stood silent.

"Come near," Ferrin beckoned him. Vius approached his master and knelt down before him. Ferrin placed his hand on Vius's head. He could feel the power immediately flow forth from the shard, vitalizing his body. As the power healed his apprentice, he could feel something within the magic. Ferrin used his mind to delve deeper into the shard, attempting to discern what it was. He was suddenly aware of several different entities. They were not bound within the shard, but connected to it.

Each of them were separate and distinct from one another. He pondered what they were, and his thoughts transferred into the shard. Immediately one of the entities responded to his thoughts. *Yes, lord?*

Ferrin separated the magic with his mind and "saw" the entities. A man dressed as a priest, a young girl, and a boy were linked to the shard. There was another entity that seemed familiar to him, but it was obscured from his vision. The old wizard didn't understand at first. Then their memories flooded him. Each of them had been touched by Broderick. Ferrin was suddenly aware of Vius in the shard's connection also.

Come forth, he called to them. Simultaneously they all answered; *Yes, lord.*

Ferrin severed the magic from his mind. He considered the implications of what he could do with such power. A grin spread across his lips. There was something specific he could do with the shard. He would make much of the shard.

Much indeed.

Chapter 16

Broderick shifted in his saddle. A throbbing soreness was climbing up his back from sitting so long. He looked over at Kira. If she was as uncomfortable as he was, she didn't show it. She was strong and fearless, which was what he loved about her. It seemed to him that she had been acting differently since his rescue. He assumed it was because of her deal with the demon that wanted their child, but there was something else he couldn't put his finger on.

It had taken them a few weeks to reach this far. Derrick had planned to travel back through Ravendale, but Kira refused to. She said it was safer to go around the city and remained adamant despite Derrick's assurance that the goblins had been cleared from the area. Derrick and his hired army had continued on through the city while Kira and himself had taken to lesser traveled roads. Broderick felt completely lost, but Kira was confident that they were going the right direction. They were rewarded earlier in the day when they ended up back on the main road.

Broderick recognized the caves they had camped near when they were first attacked by the goblins. He ran the events of the last few weeks through his mind. It seemed so long ago that they had started their journey to rescue Derrick's wife. It reminded him, painfully, of Kira's betrayal. He tried to look beyond that. He realized now that she had done what she felt was necessary to avenge her father's past crimes. He didn't agree with it, but he understood her motivation.

He still couldn't believe that Kira was carrying his child. They only had one night of passion together. Broderick reached up and scratched his chin. His face was overwhelmed with stubble and it was driving him crazy. He was accustomed to staying clean shaven and he hadn't shaved since they left. He couldn't wait to sleep in a comfortable bed again.

When they reached the outskirts of Myrwood, he almost didn't notice. His mind was running rampant. "Thank goodness," he breathed aloud. They sold their horses to the stables and entered the city on foot. Broderick was unsure where they stood. Would she come to his cousin's with him, or would she expect him to come to her place? They reached the road that led to Derrick's estate and Kira paused.

"Broderick," she said, turning to face him, "we need to talk." He nodded in agreement. "I know. Do you want to come to Derrick's with me?"

"No, you need to come with me." She clasped his hand into hers and led him through the maze of streets and through the slums of the city. He had assumed she was taking him to her house, and he was right. They entered her windowless house and she locked the door behind them. Her house was so dark it took several minutes for his eyes to adjust to the gloom. Kira didn't seem to have any problems seeing in the dark and she left him standing near the door. She disappeared into another room and then returned with an enormous book. She placed it on the table covered with flasks and other devices Broderick couldn't name.

"What is that?" he asked after he could see clearly. She motioned him to come near. "This book is a tome of demon lore," she said. "We must find a way to break my deal with the demon Skiram."

Broderick's confusion spread across his face. "Break the deal? Is that even possible?"

Kira stared at the cover of the book in silence for long moments before she met his gaze. "I don't know," she whispered softly. Her pupil-less eyes glittered with tears. "I cannot give my child to that foul creature. I won't." Her expression hardened and she clenched her fists. "I will find a way to break the deal," she swore vehemently.

"*We* will," Broderick said. "I will help you. What can I do?" he asked, reaching for the book. She slapped his hand away. "You cannot touch this book. It would suck the life from your body," she warned. "What you can do is give me the shard. It is our only hope of having even a slight chance of breaking this deal."

Broderick's heart froze. He had almost forgotten that he hadn't told her. "Kira," he said with a voice that cracked from nervousness. "I don't have it."

Kira's face scrunched up. "What? Where is it?" she demanded. The look in her eyes sent a chill up his spine. "Ferrin took it from me." For several moments he thought Kira was about to explode and unleash her wrath on him, but then she seemed to gain control of her emotions. "Why didn't you tell me this before?" she asked.

"I didn't think it was important. And what could we have done? Charged back in and gotten ourselves killed?" His shoulders slumped in defeat. "I'm sorry

I didn't tell you. It seemed we had enough to worry about, especially when the demon appeared."

She was quiet and Broderick wasn't sure what was going through her mind. Finally she sighed and opened the large book. "Perhaps we can find an answer in here."

While Kira searched through the book, Broderick walked around her house. The zombie she had showed him when they first met stood motionless in a corner, its unblinking eyes staring into oblivion. He considered going back to retrieve the shard but pushed the notion from his mind as soon as it entered. Ferrin had almost killed him even when he had the shard, so that wasn't an option.

Broderick walked over to the zombie and studied it. It seemed surreal that a corpse could be reanimated and used for tasks. He thought he saw the zombie blink, and so he stared into the corpse's eyes. A life suddenly came into the zombie's gaze and it returned his stare. Its lips parted slightly, and a whispered sound came from its mouth. Broderick didn't hear what it was, so he leaned in closer and turned his ear to the zombie's mouth.

"Seek out the *kashaph* in the Travailing Woods," the voice said. Broderick looked to Kira to see if she heard it. She was oblivious to anything but her book. He looked back to the zombie, and the voice reiterated the same thing. Broderick raised an eyebrow, wondering if he was so tired he was imagining things. The zombie laid its right hand on his chest and leaned forward. "Make haste," it said, drawing the words out slowly.

A tingling feeling began to prickle Broderick's chest where the zombie had touched him, spreading throughout his entire body. He suddenly felt weak and then his legs gave out. Darkness swallowed him.

When he came to, Kira was kneeling over him. "Are you okay?" Worry creased her brow, but her tone implied that she was irritated. "What happened?"

"I'm not sure," he answered, looking to the zombie. It was standing in the corner, lifeless and unblinking like before. "The corpse spoke to me." Kira shook her head. "That's impossible. The undead cannot speak, they can only move."

"It did move," he said. "It touched me on the chest." Broderick pulled his shirt up. A hand print was seared into his flesh. His eyes widened at the mark. Kira bit her lip. "What did it say?" she asked.

"It said to seek out the kaw-shawf," he struggled with the word, "in the Travailing Woods. What does that mean?" Kira's eyes wandered back and forth. "I've heard the word *kashaph* before, but I cannot recall where. As to the Travailing Woods … I have no idea. And this," she traced the hand print with her index finger, "this is the mark of powerful magic. Old magic. To possess another's undead creation takes a lot of energy."

Broderick shuddered. "Ferrin?" he asked.

"No. This kind of magic is older than him." Kira helped him up and led him to her bedroom. "Get some rest," she bade him. "I'm going to continue looking through the book."

He didn't argue with her. His body was weak from the magic and he was road weary. He closed his eyes and lay there for what felt like hours before he finally fell asleep.

Chapter 17

The next morning, after Broderick had eaten breakfast, he decided he needed some fresh air. Kira's house was filled with all sorts of pungent smells, some less than enjoyable. He left her studying the book and wandered about the streets. Occasionally he would look over his shoulder, taking note that the crowd of people following him steadily grew. He tried his best to ignore them so that no one would stop him and ask for a 'miracle'.

He needed somewhere to go, somewhere quiet, where he could think clearly without any distractions. He continued walking until he ducked down the street that led past the monolithic cathedral of the Church. Having lost the multitude momentarily, he paused at the gates, hesitant to enter. He hadn't been here since his parents had brought him as a child. He dismissed his uneasiness and entered the grounds.

Each church location had a name, usually referencing some important part of Raven's life. This cathedral was named St. Korban, meaning sacrifice. The church was built of thousands upon thousands of clay bricks. The front of the edifice was painted to depict the scene where Raven laid down his life, saving the world from the demonic horde that had invaded it. Surrounding the structure were several areas designed for quiet reflection. Broderick chose one that was empty and sat on the wooden bench.

He contemplated everything that had happened the last few weeks. He was so caught up in his thoughts he didn't hear the priest who came and stood behind him. When Broderick finally stood up to leave, he cried out, startled.

"My apologies," said the priest. "I didn't want to interrupt your prayers." He was an older man, perhaps in his fifties now by Broderick's guess. Though it had been over a decade since he had seen the priest, Broderick recognized him as the head of the cathedral. "It's fine," he answered. "I actually wasn't praying."

The priest raised an eyebrow. "Oh? Most people do not come out here unless they are seeking answers to questions they cannot resolve themselves. Is everything well with you?" Broderick ran his hands through his short blonde hair, sighing aloud. He considered telling the priest everything, though he decided not to share all of the details. He told the priest about his time with Kira, the feelings he had for her, and the dilemma that lay before them. "I cannot imagine handing the child over to the demon. There must be some way to break the deal."

The priest listened in silence, his face impassive and un-judging. "Life is precious," he finally said. "Were it not so, Raven would never have chosen to lay his life down to save the world. I would question why this woman—Kira, you said her name was?—would make a pact with a demon in the first place. Those vile creatures of Hell are devious and deceptive at best. I do not pass judgment, for neither she nor yourself are members of my congregation. Though if I may offer my advice, I think it would be wise of her to release any dealings with the creatures, especially with a child growing inside her.

"As to the means of breaking the deal with the demon, I'm afraid I do not know of anything. Those are dark powers she deals with, and I have no knowledge of that type of magic. We could impart a blessing on the child, but we would have to wait until the child is born."

Broderick feared as much. Everything seemed hopeless. Unless Kira found an answer in her book, it seemed that he was destined to lose the child. He thanked the priest and was about to leave when he decided to take a chance. "I have a question," he said. The priest waited for him to voice it.

"Do you know of a place called the Travailing Woods? It's not on any map I have seen, but I believe it should be." The priest seemed to consider the name. "Travailing Woods," he muttered a few times. Finally he reached up and tapped his head with his finger. "Aha! I thought I had heard the name before, and now I remember where. It is the name of a forest. Or it was. Now it is called the Divine Forest. You can find it in the east, though I do not know why you would want to go there."

"Why not?" Broderick asked.

"It is desolate of any life. Priests of old use to believe that there were many gods, and that they stood in that very forest when they created the living things of the world. During the war with the demons, a great dragon burst forth from under the forest. A large section of the forest died from the destruction the beast caused, and as a result, even animals no longer desire to live there. An unholy power stained the land. The forest is still there, though it slowly dies."

A spark of hope lit up inside of Broderick. If the voice that spoke through the zombie told him to go to the Travailing Woods, then perhaps there was something there that could help him. Kira said the magic was powerful, older than Ferrin. If the magic was as strong as the shard, maybe they could find a way to use it to break the deal with the demon.

"Thank you," Broderick said appreciatively. He left the priest and returned to the street. He was going to return back to Kira's, but instead he decided to go see his cousin. He navigated the crowded roads and eventually made it to the gates of Derrick's estate. He was about to pass through the entry when he heard a noise from some bushes on the outside of the gate. He walked over and saw a form sitting on the ground.

"What did you do to my child?" a wretched and tearful voice asked. Broderick wasn't sure he heard correctly. He knelt down beside the person, a woman, and leaned in. Her face was covered in tears and dirt. Her eyes had a madness in them that threatened to consume him. "What did you do to my child!" she screamed at him. She flailed weakly, trying to strike him. He fell back out of the way. "What are you talking about?" he asked.

"You! You changed him! You changed my son. He looks like my son, but he isn't my child! He is evil!" the woman wailed on and on, groaning the same statements like a crazed monotony.

"She's been here for a week," said one of the guards, approaching from behind. Broderick looked to the soldier and stood up, brushing dust from the road off his pants. "What is she talking about? Is she okay?" The guard shrugged. "I don't know. We've told her if she doesn't leave by nightfall, we'll have to escort her from the estate."

As Broderick stared at her, realization struck him. She was the mother of the boy he had healed. He studied her face intently. *That's her all right.* He knelt down beside her again. "What do you mean your son is evil?" he asked, hoping that she was not completely overcome with madness. She stared down at the ground, running her fingers in the dirt. "He started doing things. Odd things. It didn't seem like anything to worry about …" she trailed off, her fingers pausing in the dirt. "And then he *changed* … he killed the dog with a knife. And then he turned it on me." Her reddened eyes met his. "I took it from him, but he … he … he ran away. I don't know where he is."

A chill ran up Broderick's spine. *What if the magic was flawed?* Without saying another word, he left the woman with the guard and trudged up the path to his cousin's villa. It was as peaceful and serene as it was when he had left to find Octavia. He found Derrick in the atrium, drinking honeysuckle and going over various missives. Derrick raised his eyes and smiled broadly. "Cousin! I was wondering when you'd arrive. Come, take a seat." Broderick sat at the table with his cousin and a servant poured him a glass of the sweet nectar.

"How was the journey back? Not too trying, I hope?"

Broderick shook his head. "No, it was fine. The woman at your gates seems to blame me for her son going crazy." He took a drink from the cup the servant gave him and waited for his cousin to respond. Derrick waved it away. "The soldiers will deal with her, don't worry about that."

"I fear I did something wrong, though I don't know what. How is Claire? Is she … normal?" Derrick laughed. "Of course she is! And we have you to thank for that. Now that my wife is home safe I can turn my attention back to the matters of business." Derrick waved at the papers covering the table. "Do you see these? These are orders for honeysuckle. Do you know how much money I am going to make? More than any previous year!"

Broderick grinned at his cousin's excitement. "That's great, Derrick. I am happy for you."

"And I have been thinking, cousin. I could use some help around here. I could front you the money to buy your own land here in the city and you could work for me. What do you say?" Broderick opened his mouth to answer, but he didn't know what to say. "Derrick, I would love to accept your generous offer, but there is something I must do before I can consider doing anything else."

"What is it? I can have a servant handle it for you."

Broderick released everything. He shared how he felt for Kira, their night of passion on the road, her betrayal, her violent father, and their unborn child. He broke down and cried, telling his cousin every detail. He told him about Ferrin taking the shard, and that it seemed the only answer lay in traveling to the east to seek out whoever, or whatever, had spoken to him through the zombie.

Derrick remained silent through it all. When Broderick finished the tale, Derrick leaned back in his chair and crossed his arms. "She's bewitched you," he said grimly. Broderick protested vehemently.

"Yes, yes she has. Why else would you abandon everything you've known to go gallivanting off to some forest to search for God knows what?"

"Because I love her."

Derrick shook his head. "Cousin, I know you cannot see it because you are so close to the situation, but she is playing you for whatever she can get. I cannot, nor will I try, to stop you. But mark my words well. This will not end favorably for you."

"You don't understand," Broderick said defensively. "She has not bewitched me. She wants the same thing I do, and that is to save the life of our child from that demon. Nothing more. If you don't want to help me find a way, so be it. But I have wasted enough time already and I must go as soon as possible."

Derrick waved his hand. "You know I will help you in any way I can. You went to find my wife. Take whatever supplies you need. If you need soldiers, talk with my Captain. I'll approve everything." Broderick rose from the chair and clasped hands with his cousin. "Thank you, Derrick. I'll repay you when this is all over."

"Please," Derrick snorted derisively, "Don't insult my generosity. Just promise me one thing."

"What's that?"

"That you will return alive."

Broderick grinned. "I'll do my best."

Chapter 18

The next morning, just before sunrise, Broderick and a troop of five soldiers left Myrwood heading east. They each rode a swift mount and followed the same road he had taken with Kira, planning to bypass Ravendale without stopping. He had no desire to see Morell again. The place also reminded him of Kira's betrayal, and he would just as soon forget about it.

The soldiers were lively and excited to be on the road. They each took turns telling Broderick stories of war and battle, and especially of their own epics. Broderick enjoyed their company and was glad his cousin insisted on sending them along. He initially had decided to go alone, but he was glad that he didn't. Having them to talk to and keep him company made the miles go by faster.

"I love working for Lord Derrick, but we are all adventurous. Opportunities like this help break up the monotony. We're also fattening up standing around and guarding the fields. This will give us the chance to re-hone our skills. Do you know how to handle a blade?" One of the soldiers, Marc, asked.

"I know a little," Broderick admitted, "though not enough to defend myself against someone trained like yourself. I'm a woodsman by trade and have never had the need to learn."

"We must change that," Marc winked. "I'll train you myself."

As the hours passed, he learned a considerable amount about the soldiers he traveled with. Marc was the leader of the small unit. He looked young, but his features belied his age. He was in his late thirties, with brown hair cut in the current style of middle class citizens. He wore a drab brown tunic under a shirt of chain mail, trousers of a similar color, and black leather boots. His experience in warfare was substantial, having been a soldier since he was eighteen. He had served under a few lords who sought to expand their holdings, aided in several of the attempts to drive the goblins from the hills where he and Kira had been attacked, and had been chosen to oversee the defenses for Myrwood.

There was also Ged, an older fellow. Broderick guessed the man to be in his sixties. He stood over six feet in height. His head was bald, but he sported a thick gray beard that hung past his neck. He wore a tan leather cuirass and brown pants, as well as the same black leather boots as Marc. He carried a claymore which measured over four feet long. The sword had a cross-guard that consisted of two downward-curving arms and two large, round, concave plates that protected the fore-grip, resembling an open clam. He may have been the oldest of the five, but Broderick had no doubts that Ged was just as deadly as the others.

Joel was the youngest, having just had his nineteenth birthday. He was Marc's apprentice, studying under him to learn battle tactics and warfare. He was from a wealthy family of a city Broderick had never heard of. He would train under Marc for another two years and then return home to take up arms for the city's Lord. His armor was similar to Ged's, but he wore chain mail under his cuirass. He claimed it was too heavy and made it hard to move, but Marc insisted on him wearing it to condition his body.

The other two, Callow and Ewan, were brothers. Callow was the elder of the two, but Ewan was the more experienced and had recruited his brother into the military life. They likely could have passed as twins for they so resembled one another, but Callow was a year older. They were both blonde, with the same style haircut as Marc. Both were evenly matched in height, but Ewan was by far the more muscular. They each wore a leather cuirass like Ged's, but Callow's was a shiny polished black hue, and Ewan's was silver. Their armor was emblazoned with their family crest on the chest; a griffin standing on its back legs holding a red flag in its beak. Callow wielded a battleax while Ewan favored a flamberge.

"We shall make camp at dusk, if that is well with you?" Marc asked Broderick. "Indeed it is," Broderick answered. He would be glad to finally get some rest. When they stopped for the night, they had left the caves that housed the goblins a fair distance behind them. Ged and the two brothers had stopped to run a quick search through some of the hollows, but didn't come across any of the vile creatures.

After they met back up with Broderick and the others, they set about laying out bedrolls and building a fire. They ate a small meal that consisted of bread and rabbit, which Callow had caught in the caves. Marc set the order of who was to stand watch, and the rest laid down to sleep. Broderick closed his eyes but sleep eluded him. He thought about Kira and the dilemma they faced. He truly hoped that he would find a way to save the baby. He was unaware of how long it was before he finally fell asleep. His dreams were filled with eerie scenes and monsters rampaging across the land, slaughtering children.

His eyes shot open as he awoke suddenly. Marc was standing over him, the hint of a grin tugging at his lips. "Ready for your first lesson?" he asked.

Broderick sat up and looked around. Everyone was already up and ready to get back on the road. "Rise early often?" Broderick returned, rising out of bed with a grunt. "That's the life," Marc answered. "Eat and prepare yourself."

"For what?"

"Sword lessons."

—

Sweat rolled down Broderick's face. The morning was cool, but the physical exertion was brutal. Marc was a great teacher, though he showed no mercy and didn't give Broderick a break. "Water," Broderick gasped after an intense flurry of blades. "There are no breaks in war," Marc replied. He came at Broderick again, slashing and twirling so gracefully Broderick doubted he would ever be as adept as the soldier.

"This isn't war," Broderick returned, breathing heavily. He dropped his sword to the ground. "I give." Marc laughed and sheathed his own blade. "You are a quick learner. You should be proud of yourself. Even Joel couldn't defend as well as you after his first few months of training."

Broderick retrieved his water skin from his mount. He splashed some on his face then drank deeply. He stripped his shirt off and wiped his face. Folding the shirt, he stashed it in a pouch on his saddle. "We're ready if you are," Marc said. Broderick shook his head in disbelief. "You don't need a break?"

Marc smiled and was about to answer, but Broderick waved his hand and said, "I know, I know. There are no breaks in war."

"You're a quick learner," Marc said again.

Broderick climbed onto his horse and they got back onto the road. "Where exactly is this forest?" he asked Marc. The soldier pulled a map out from his saddle and unrolled it. "It is further east that I have been. It is roughly a few hours from the Citadel."

Broderick raised his eyebrow. "As in, *the* Citadel? Where Raven died?" Marc nodded. "The same. Like I said, it's farther east than I have been. It shouldn't be hard to find, as the map shows the main road passing next to the forest. It should take us two weeks at this pace. I think it would do us well to stay at any inns we pass. When our supplies run low, we will need to replenish them, and I have found inns to offer the best deals. If you would like to stop anywhere, just let me know."

"No, no. I would like to get there as quickly as possible. Your plan is fine with me, so long as we aren't wasting time anywhere. Unfortunately, this journey isn't for leisure. I cannot explain why. I hope you understand?"

"No need to explain. We are here for your protection. Whatever your desire, we shall do."

Broderick was satisfied with that answer. He couldn't wait for the two weeks to come and go. Time at this point, in his opinion, was the most valuable commodity. And it didn't feel like he had enough.

—

As the days blurred together, Broderick began to think less of his problems. The soldiers were constantly talking with him, which kept him from drawing into the dark depths of his mind. Marc also continued teaching him in the art of the sword. They passed through many small towns, including the town where Broderick had listened to the old man who had seen the wizard. In the back of his mind, Broderick feared that Ferrin would show himself and try to kill him.

He knew it was a foolish thought, but he had seen the crazed look in Ferrin's eyes. *That man is capable of so much,* he thought. They passed through the town without incident, however. The road forked, north toward Eurn where Ferrin's fortress resided, the other east toward their goal. As they traveled further in the direction of the forest, the towns became further spaced apart until eventually, there were no signs of civilization at all.

"The map shows three towns we should have passed through. Did we possibly miss another road?" Marc asked aloud. Broderick thought about it and decided he hadn't seen any other path. He said as much to Marc. They continued on despite their reservations. After another mile, Broderick noticed flowing water. It turned into a stream that ran along the right side of the road. They stopped to let their mounts drink and to refresh themselves in the shallow water. Marc was studying the map again with a puzzled look on his face.

Broderick walked over to the soldier and peered at the map with him. "What is it?" he asked.

Marc pointed to a line on the map. "This is the road we are on. Here," he pointed to another line which ran alongside of the first, "is the stream that we see before us. And this," he moved his finger to a darkened circle, "is a town that should be where we are standing. This doesn't make any sense."

Broderick looked up from the map and surveyed their surroundings. Marc was right. There should be a town, or at least a village, but there was nothing. "I don't even see remnants of buildings," Broderick said. "How old is that map?"

Marc flipped the map over and viewed the inscription. "It was drawn up a year ago," he answered. "That can't be right," he added. "How could everything just disappear in a year?" Broderick shrugged. He didn't have an answer to that. They ate a small meal and continued their trek. Broderick lost himself in his thoughts as they traveled on, thinking about his home in the woods and the repairs he needed to make. *Perhaps Kira will want to live there with me.*

Broderick was awakened from his reverie when he noticed they had stopped. His own horse had even ceased going forward. "What is it?" he asked, looking about. No one answered, but after a moment he realized the same thing. There was no sound. No birds sang. No crickets chirped. It was almost as if the wind itself didn't move. Everything was still.

"This place is cursed," Ged muttered under his breath.

No one said anything, and Broderick wondered if Ged was right. The horses seemed reluctant to go forward, but finally conceded to their master's urgings. The landscape changed dramatically. Where there should have been vibrant trees there were only dead stumps. The soil was blackened as if it had been burned. Finally the horses refused to go any further. They all dismounted. The stream had turned to a dull red color and no fish could be seen. Chills crept up Broderick's flesh, making him involuntarily cringe.

He knelt down and pressed his finger into the black soil and then held it up before his eyes. It was not ash. It was black dirt. He stood back up and brushed his finger off on his pants. They all stood in silence, looking around at the dead landscape.

"What could cause such destruction?" Broderick asked, barely speaking above a whisper. Marc shook his head slowly in answer.

"Where are we?"

In response, Marc handed the map over to him. Broderick looked it over and shook his head in disbelief. "This is the Divine Forest," he answered himself aloud.

Chapter 19

"This place is cursed," Ged said again. The old soldier lifted his hand and traced a symbol in the air to ward off evil spirits. The others looked around balefully, and Broderick got the feeling they didn't want to be there anymore than he did.

"I think we should travel further into the tree line," Broderick said, pointing. "The entire forest can't be dead." All but Marc shook their heads in disagreement. Marc led his horse over to one of the blackened trees and tied the reins to one of the few branches that seemed sturdy. Then he turned and addressed them. "Let's move it," he ordered. Grabbing his arming sword from the saddle, he strapped the sheath around his waist. With a nod to Broderick, he walked forth into the woods.

Broderick admired the man's courage. He looked to the other soldiers, smiled, and then followed after Marc. After a few minutes, he could hear them following. The sound of snapping twigs and crunching leaves echoed loudly in the silence. They traveled for the better part of an hour before they stopped to rest. The air was foul and made breathing difficult. Broderick perused the map again, wishing there was some way to know if they were heading in the right direction. Sweat dripped down his face. His eyes and throat burned like fire.

He noticed Marc was kneeling down, examining something in the dirt. Broderick walked over and waited for him to speak. The soldier ran his hand through his sweat-soaked hair and stood up. "This used to be a path," he said. "It forks and runs two different directions. The map doesn't show this path."

Broderick studied the ground as well. "What should we do?" he asked.

Marc shrugged, the clink of his chain mail seeming extremely loud. "Should we split up?" Broderick asked. He scratched his chin and stared into the dead trees, uncertain. "Seems the best course to me," Marc answered. "Though I don't think they will agree." He nodded toward the other soldiers.

"It can't be helped," Broderick said absently. He could hear a humming sound in his ears. It was faint, but unmistakable. "Joel, Callow, and Ewan. You three will take the path that leads left. Ged, you will accompany me and Broderick to the right. Assuming the paths don't reconnect an hour further in, we shall circle back and meet here and determine what to do then. Otherwise, we'll see each other on the path."

There was a moment of silence as they all stared at each other. Then, without any words, they grouped together and set out on the different paths. "Do you hear anything?" Broderick asked, looking around at the dead trees. The humming was constant, repeating the same pattern over and over.

"Hear what?" Ged grunted. Marc shook his head. *That's odd,* thought Broderick. They continued following the trail. It was covered with dead leaves and almost obscured entirely by the elements. Every so often, Marc would brush the compost aside with his boot to ensure they were still traveling on it. Broderick found it hard to think clearly with the continuous noise in his ears. He furiously rubbed the skin around his ear with his finger, thinking that perhaps it wasn't a real sound.

It continued. And as they walked deeper into the woods, the sound got louder. It was progressive, steadily growing in volume until it was as though someone were talking at a normal pitch directly into his ear. It became less of a general hum and began to sound like words. They were not words he had ever heard before. They were foreign to him, but they evoked pictures in his mind.

Images of tall, strong, beautiful trees with vibrant colors invaded his psyche. Healthy animals leaping through shrubbery assaulted him. Nourishing soil fed the foliage. And there was something else. Blurred images of … forms … walking in the background of the images. Broderick couldn't make out what or who they were. There was a deep sadness attached to the images. He felt it as if he had known these things and they were now gone, lost forever in the past. His eyes watered with the emotional churnings.

And then, suddenly, the images and the humming stopped. Broderick froze mid-step he was so surprised. Marc and Ged looked at him quizzically. Broderick shook his head, as if waking from a dream and continued on. The ground rose before them, a small hill that they easily topped. And then they froze. There, at the bottom of the hill and reaching as far as they could see, was life. Massive trees towered overhead. Their trunks were so wide, Broderick doubted twenty men could connect arms around them.

The leaves glittered in the light, bright emeralds alight with fire inside them. They could hear the sounds of animals, and the wind gently rocked the branches of the trees. *This is a forest as it should be.*

They descended the hill slowly, gazing up at the trees in awe. Broderick couldn't believe how big the trees were. They were much larger than the ones he normally cut down for lumber. And the leaves didn't seem normal to him. As they reached the bottom of the hill, one of the leaves fell off a branch and slowly swirled down to the ground. Broderick knelt down and picked it up, marveling at its beauty.

And he was right. They weren't normal. It was as light as a normal leaf, but it was hard as a rock. It *was* a rock! Broderick held it up for Marc to see. "It's an emerald!" he exclaimed. Marc took it and investigated the claim himself. His eyes widened in disbelief. "How?"

Broderick was just as speechless and could only shake his head in answer. "That one leaf could fetch a price," Ged hinted. "Makes you wonder what else is in there." They exchanged looks. "Do we dare?" Marc asked.

Broderick rose back to his feet. "We haven't come this far for nothing. If you don't want to follow, you don't have to."

"There is a problem. Joel and the brothers will suspect ill if we don't return," just as Marc finished his sentence, they heard someone approaching. Joel staggered onto the path from the side of the living forest and dropped to the ground. Marc rushed over to the young soldier. "He's alive. I don't see any wounds," he added after turning Joel onto his back.

Joel sat up, gasping. "They were captured!" he shouted over and over. Broderick watched in fear as

Marc tried to calm him. "Who was captured?" Marc asked.

"The brothers!"

"Who took them?" Marc demanded.

"I don't know. I couldn't see them. They were too fast … too fast," he mumbled.

Marc looked at Broderick. "We must find them. I don't know what you have come here for, nor do I care. But I will not leave my men behind."

"I would never ask you to," Broderick replied. "Let us go and find them."

Ged helped Joel to his feet. Drawing his sword, Marc took the lead, followed by Broderick, Joel, and then Ged. They walked cautiously, unsure of who they might be dealing with. Less than a hundred paces into the woods and Marc paused, motioning them to be still. Broderick listened intently, but he didn't notice anything out of the ordinary.

Then Marc looked up into the trees. Broderick followed suit and was stunned to see forms moving among the branches. He almost couldn't see them, for their cloaks made them blend into their surroundings quite deceptively. But they were there. And they were armed.

Several of them held bows up, arrows nocked and ready to fire. One of them, Broderick assumed the leader, stepped out from the others. "Turn and go back from where you came," the voice was obviously male, but it sounded like music to Broderick.

"I am looking for my men," Marc returned. "Have you seen them?"

The figure tilted his head and Broderick thought he saw a glimpse of long hair hidden beneath the figure's hood. "They are with you?" he asked.

"They are."

"Then you are all trespassers and must pay the price. Cut them down," he ordered. The others lifted their bows and drew back their strings.

"I seek the *kashaph*!" Broderick shouted.

That caused the figures to hesitate. "The *kashaph*? How do you know of the *kashaph*?" The leader dropped nimbly to the ground from the tree, easily landing on his feet. He kept his distance and reiterated his question. Broderick eased the troubled look on Marc's face by patting him on the shoulder.

"I was told to seek out the *kashaph* in the Travailing Woods," he said. "And so here I am. These men are my guards. This is the Travailing Woods, is it not?"

The leader bowed low. "This is indeed. We will allow you to enter our domain, but we cannot allow these armed men to enter of their own accord."

"Then they shall wait for my return outside of the woods."

The figure shook his head and raised his hand up, palm outward, and said, "*Yashin*!" Broderick turned to see Marc, Ged, and Joel's bodies slump to the ground. At first, he thought they were dead. But then he saw that they were breathing. "What did you do to them?" he demanded angrily. A gust of wind swept through the branches suddenly, blowing the figure's hood back. Broderick's anger dissipated as quickly as it flared. Pale skin, long hair, and pointed ears greeted him.

He was gazing at a thing of legend, a creature only heard of in ancient tales.

He was staring at an elf.

Chapter 20

"They are sleeping," the elf said calmly, unperturbed by his anger. "Do not worry about them. They are safe here. Follow me," the elf turned and began to walk through the trees. Broderick hesitantly followed. The elf's movements were graceful and fluid. Not even the dead leaves on the forest floor crunched under his feet. As they walked, Broderick became aware of more elves among the trees.

The trees served as their homes, as best as he could guess. There were no doors, but many trees had curved archways leading into them. He marveled as elves came and went, walking into and out of the massive trees. They were all dressed similar to his guide, wearing dark greens and browns. "What is your name?" Broderick asked.

Without looking back, the elf laughed. It was a beautiful sound in his ears. "You humans haven't changed much. Names are powerful things, and we don't give them to strangers." The answer reminded him of Kira. As they moved deeper into the forest, Broderick noticed more and more elves. Fragrant smells welcomed him, enticing him to come and see where they originated. Children ran here and there, their laughter just as musical as his guide's. "This is our city," the elf said, waving his hand.

"Do you have many cities?" Broderick asked, awed by the beauty of everything he saw. "No." When he answered, the elf's tone had changed, and Broderick could feel a deep sadness behind the word.

"Before we got here, we passed through an area that looked burned. What happened there?"

The elf stopped and turned to face him. "You talk much," he said. "You ask too many questions. Can you not be content without the need to know everything? How does the eagle soar on the wind? How does the bear know when it is time to hibernate? Have you asked questions such as these before? Do you ponder over such matters?"

Broderick was taken aback. "No," he answered. "I have not wondered about those things."

"I suspected not. You only want answers to your own questions, and nothing else. That, human, is why your race is selfish and undeserving."

Broderick could only gape at the elf in shock. He didn't get angry, for when he thought about it, there much truth to what he said. At least there was truth in it for him. He knew his quest to save his baby was selfish, especially when someone like Ferrin had the shard.

"I apologize," the elf said suddenly, bowing to him. "I let my emotions force my words. Come, we are getting close."

They continued down the path that led through the elven city and beyond. The sights and smells had long faded and Broderick began to wonder what the elf meant by close when the path abruptly ended. Without slowing, the elf continued forth. As soon as he stepped off the end of the path, he disappeared from sight. Broderick blinked. Was he seeing things, or had the elf simply vanished?

"Are you coming?" the elf's voice rang out.

"Coming where?"

Nothing. Broderick looked around and shook his head. Nothing made sense anymore. Walking forward, he stopped at the edge of the path. There was nothing but trees for as far as he could see. Shrugging, he stepped off the path.

Only he didn't step into trees. Broderick was surrounded by the same dead forest he passed through earlier. His guide stood there, watching. Broderick was confused. Was he back at the beginning of the forest?

"Where are we?" he asked.

"This is the home of the *kashaph*. I must leave you now, but he will be here shortly. Don't wander," the elf warned, "for this place is beyond the safety of our woods." The elf bowed to him again and disappeared back the way they had come.

Broderick stood still and listened. There was no sound, just like before. The once mighty trees were black and twisted. The soil was also black and a heavy stench of death pervaded the air. He wondered where he was, and where was this *kashaph* that he was trying to find?

A sound nearby turned his attention to the shadows in a gathering of dead trees to the left. He leaned his head out, straining to see what made the noise. He saw something move, darting from one side of the trees to the other. *Is that a dog?*

Howling sounded through the air, causing the hairs on his arms to stand on end. From the shadows emerged a pack of wolves. Broderick back-stepped quickly, looking around for something he could defend himself with. He cursed the elves for taking the sword Marc had given him. Seeing a thick branch, he stooped down and grabbed it, bringing it to bear in front of him. He clenched the branch tight and felt it crumble in his hands.

He threw the remains down as he watched the wolves. Something about them didn't seem right. Their fur was mangled, with entire spots missing completely. Their eyes glowed with a bloodlust Broderick couldn't begin to fathom. One of the wolves growled at him, an unearthly sound. And then it sprinted forward, leaping into the air straight at him.

Instinctively he threw his arms up and closed his eyes, bracing his body for the impact. A sizzling sound filled his ears. He waited for the fangs and the claws, but nothing happened. Opening his eyes, he saw a figure clothed in black standing to his right. The wolf that had leapt at him lay dead. The other wolves were gathering around the figure, baring their teeth and growling ferociously.

One of the wolves tried to attack only to be burned by some invisible barrier. It yelped and retreated. The other wolves didn't shrink back. They circled the figure, trying to find a weakness. The wolf that retreated seemed to remember Broderick was there, and it began to stalk toward him. Broderick was so enrapt, he didn't notice. The wolf attacked him, snapping at his legs. Broderick cried out in surprise and kicked at the wolf.

Undaunted, the wolf pressed its attack, trying to force Broderick to lose his footing. A jagged blue light forked out from the figure and blasted the wolf, killing it instantly. Broderick turned his attention back to the figure and watched in horror as the remaining wolves attacked, burying the figure beneath their bodies, snapping and growling.

The overwhelming urge to turn and flee assaulted his mind, and he almost obeyed. All of a sudden, the mass of wolf bodies bulged upward three times before all of them were flung into the air. Several fist-sized balls of white flame shot out from the figure's hands, hurtling through the air and striking each wolf, setting them ablaze. The pungent smells of burnt hair and flesh assaulted Broderick, almost making him vomit.

He coughed and covered his nose in a pitiful attempt to blot out the smell. The black clothed figure approached him. "Who are you?" Broderick asked.

"I am Nae'fir," the elf answered. "And you must be Broderick, the woodsman turned healer." The elf pulled his hood back to reveal the same features as all the other elves he had seen. The delicate bone structure, the pointed ears, and the long hair. Nae'fir's hair was a rich golden brown. His skin was pale, probably the whitest elf Broderick had seen yet. His eyes were a light blue, almost gray.

"Were those wolves?" he asked.

Nae'fir nodded. "Yes. Or at least they used to be, before the plague took them."

"The plague?"

Nae'fir motioned him to follow. "It never ceases to amaze me at how quickly humans forget the past. It has only been eighty years, after all." The elf led him to a tree that had an arched entryway carved into it. Speaking words Broderick didn't understand,

Nae'fir waved his hand over the doorway. A luminescent glow came to life briefly, then disappeared.

The elf led him into the tree. Broderick half expected to find it hard to maneuver inside the tree. He couldn't have been more wrong. The size of the tree on the outside belied what lay within. A massive open space greeted him. The ceiling could not be seen for the height. A table large enough to seat twenty people, a long wall of shelves covered in books, and many other things surprised Broderick.

"This tree doesn't seem like it is big enough to hold all of this," Broderick said.

Nae'fir smiled at him. "Nothing in the Travailing Woods is as it seems. The space inside the trees is enhanced by magic. Would you like something to drink? Or something to eat, perhaps?"

"I wouldn't mind some water," Broderick answered. Nae'fir bade him to sit at the table and went to a cabinet and retrieved two wooden mugs. Broderick picked a chair at random and sat down. He had yet to grasp everything he had seen so far.

Nae'fir brought the mugs to the table and set one before Broderick before taking a seat himself. "I assume you have many questions. I will certainly answer them if I can, but I first must ask my own question."

Broderick nodded. He took a sip from the mug and a sound of pleasure escaped his lips. "This is good. What is it?"

"We call it *shekhar.* We boil the roots of dandelions in water. It is sweet to drink, but we drink it for other reasons as well." Nae'fir paused, sipped from his own mug, and looked directly at Broderick. "My question is this: do you still have the shard that fell from the sky?"

Broderick shook his head. "No, I don't. It was taken from me by a wizard. How do you know who I am? And how do you know about the shard?"

"There is not much that escapes our notice," Nae'fir answered. "And I also saw the shard the night it fell to the earth. You say a wizard took it from you. Do you know the name of this wizard?"

"Ferrin."

Nae'fir sat back in his chair, a slight scowl on his face. "I should have known."

"You know him?" Broderick asked. He took another sip of the drink.

"I know *of* him. While I have never met him, I think I have gathered enough to know what he seeks to do. The artifact he holds is no mere trinket. With the right knowledge, there are countless things it can be used for. Do you know where this wizard is?"

"No. He has a castle in Eurn, but we didn't wait around to see if he would kill us or not. He may still be there."

"I doubt that," Nae'fir said.

"I have to admit, I did not think elves really existed. I've heard mention in songs and old stories, but I am having trouble understanding that this is all real and not something I am dreaming. I'm not dreaming, am I?"

"I'm afraid not. We never used to be so reclusive. Our race has always lived in this forest, as far back as history teaches us. As the years passed, we were often targeted by human raiding parties. I suppose our secrets drove them to commit the acts they did. I honestly don't know." Nae'fir stared into his mug. "Our king decided that to ensure the safety of our people, we should break communication with the world.

"It was a controversial decision to say the least. There were many who opposed it. Some didn't believe that was the answer. Others … they had taken love interests in humans and had even married. Once the king decided to close the borders of the forest, more decisions had to be made. What happened if humans mistakenly entered our cities? Did we kill them? What about those elves who had married humans? Did we cast the elves out, or allow the humans to stay?"

Broderick listened intently. "What secrets were the humans, my people, after?"

Nae'fir sighed. "We have many secrets. What exactly they wanted, we don't know. The king, after many objections, finally sealed the forest off from the outside world. So long as no one came with the intent to harm, they would be left alone. And for centuries we flourished. Then the war with the demons happened. Our king said it was punishment on the humans for their wrongdoing.

"Not everyone agreed with him on that subject, either. Including me. He refused to give aid to the humans. And the demons eventually made it this far. We killed them without much challenge. Then the Beast of the Earth came forth, eighty years ago, and left a plague on our forest. It is an evil magic that has killed our beloved forest."

"All the blackened trees and soil, that's not from fire? That's from the dragon that rose from the forest?"

Nae'fir nodded. "I see your people remember the invasion, at least. That is good. One must learn from the past, else he will make the same mistakes. No, the deadness that sweeps through our forest is not from fire. It is a plague, a blight that does not stop. Our way of life is threatened. You see, our life-force is tied to the forest. As it dies, we die. We have stalled the plague from furthering, but we cannot hold it off forever. Not without help."

Realization flooded through Broderick. "You want the shard," he reasoned. "You believe it is strong enough to stop the plague?"

Nae'fir smiled wanly. "I do."

"Is that why you asked me to come here?"

"It is the main reason, yes, but not the only reason. I cannot find the shard without your help, but I know that you also seek something. I have asked you here to propose an arrangement. If you help me retrieve the shard, I will help you break the deal your lover made with the demon."

"You can do that?" Broderick asked, stunned.

Nae'fir nodded. "I can. A task like that is easy for one like me. But you must help me first. The lives of my people are at stake."

Broderick shook his head. "I would love to help you, but I don't know how I can. I don't know where Ferrin is or where he might have taken the shard."

"Let me see your palm," he said. Broderick laid his hands on the table and displayed the inside of his hands. Nae'fir placed his index finger into Broderick's right palm, where the shard had burned him when he first found it.

The skin had been burned to the bone and until recently, was open. After Ferrin had taken the shard, skin had begun to grow over the painless wound. When Nae'fir touched it, a burning sensation coursed through his arm and the skin peeled away to reveal the bone again.

"This," Nae'fir said, "is a bonding scar. Though you may not have the shard, you can still use the powers of the shard if you focus enough. The magic chose you, Broderick. With your connection, you can locate the shard and we can retrieve it."

"How did the magic choose me? And even if I could do that, how would we defeat Ferrin? I have seen what he is capable of!"

"Calm yourself. I will deal with Ferrin when the time comes. And magic is not something that we use as a tool. Magic is not some mystical force. Magic is. And it has chosen you for a reason. What that reason is I cannot say. It is up to you to find that out. My people and your child do not have the time for you to be fearful of the unknown. Action must be taken, and it must be taken now. What say you, Broderick? Will you help me so that in turn I may help you?"

Broderick ran his hands over his face and through his hair. This was big. Too big. This was not something he felt he could do, nor something that he wanted to do. But if Nae'fir was being honest, if the elf could break the deal with the demon …

"You have my word. I will help you."

Chapter 21

Gray walls of stone rose up from the mountain side, jagged and worn with age. Ferrin stood in the ruins of what was once a sprawling courtyard. Most of the walls were still intact, with arched doorways that separated various rooms and chambers. Ferrin shuffled along, his staff bearing his weight. The place once had beautiful vaulted ceilings, but after countless ages the ceilings had crumbled and were gone, replaced with a clear view of the sky.

Ferrin had both the sword *Sorandra* and the shard from the sun that he had stolen from Broderick. His trusted apprentice Vius walked behind him, carrying the sword. Ferrin himself held the shard. While he trusted Vius more than any of his other apprentices, he didn't trust him with the shard. Sometimes power could not be given to another.

It had taken nearly three weeks for them to reach the ruins. The Starforge Mountains were hundreds of miles from the frozen lands of Eurn, and for unknown reasons, magic could not be used to travel to them. Many speculated as to why, but none knew for sure. Ferrin's body was wasting away as it was, and the journey was especially hard on him. The shard had given him a feeling of being refreshed, but it was not enough. He wanted to see the full extent of what the shard could do.

And the one place that he thought could reveal its strength was here. Ferrin paused to run his hands along the marble pillars. Some of the stones crumbled at his touch. He could tell that no magic had been used to create the ancient stone fortress. Even long after magic faded, there was always a residual energy left behind. Ferrin didn't feel any in this place. He marveled at the great lengths it must have taken to build the fortress. Many men had probably died in their attempts to bring the stones up the mountains. The gray marble that comprised almost the entirety of the place was rare and found only near the Great Sea.

Ferrin had amassed a great wealth of knowledge, but even he did not know who was responsible for its construction. The old wizard stared out at the mountain range, the tall peaks stretching as far as he could see. This was a place of strength, of ancient history, and of powerful magic. The fortress had not been built by magic, but Ferrin could feel it in the mountains. Old magic from a time long before his own.

He withdrew the shard from a pocket within his robes and clutched it tightly in his hand. Closing his eyes, he sent his consciousness flowing into the stone. He could feel the power wash over him like waves crashing onto a shore. He savored the feeling for a moment before searching out the threads of light that were the consciousness' of those whose lives were bound within the shard.

He found Morell, the head of the priests in Ravendale. Ferrin sent his thoughts toward his glowing thread. *Have you done as I asked?*

A pause ensued, and then: *I have.*

Good. I have another task for you. Send a contingent of twenty priests to the Starforge Mountains. They must be devout in their faith, unwavering. Men unlike yourself. There are ruins of an ancient structure hidden in the peaks, do you know them?

I do.

Send them here to me immediately. Have you tracked down the traitor yet?

Morell's thread pulsed and flared brightly for a moment, then resumed its normal glow. *No, Master. I believe I am close to finding him, however.*

Good. Do not forget to alert me when you do. Ferrin severed the mental link with the priest and searched for the thread of the young girl. *Claire,* he called out to her.

Yes?, she answered.

Have you heard any word on your uncle?

No, Master.

Ferrin allowed his irritation to travel through the thread so that she knew he was displeased. *Search harder. Have you tried to approach the Necromancer?*

Yes, Master. She remains hidden from me, but I do not think she is aware of my ... circumstances.

Try harder! he made his fury evident to her, then severed the connection. He pushed his mind through the shard, trying to find the thread of consciousness that seemed out of his reach. He could feel it on the fringes of the shard, but he still could not make a mental connection to it.

Frustrated, he abandoned the attempt and retracted his mind from the shard. He hid the stone back within his robes and turned to Vius. The apprentice stood unmoving before him. "Prepare the ritual," he commanded. "It will take the priests some time to get here, but we need everything in place. Once we begin, we will have to move quickly. When the priests realize what is happening, they will not stand idle."

Vius nodded in silence and set about as he was instructed. Ferrin turned his gaze back out toward the towering mountain peaks. Located within the mountain, at the end of the courtyard, there was a cave. It was no ordinary cave as Ferrin had discovered many years before. In his continual quest for power, he had found many artifacts and many strange places. He shuffled across the courtyard and entered the cave.

It was formed naturally, but that was perhaps the only natural thing about it. The walls of the cave were inscribed with drawings and runes. The many drawings depicted strange creatures, some of which Ferrin recognized from Hell. The runes, after long hours of translation, were spells of all types: bindings and summonings, divinations and transmutations, enchantments and illusions, and even necromancy.

There was one spell in particular that had caught his attention. He moved to stand before the runes of the spell, reading over it again. It required a massive amount of holy blood, or blood of priests, an item of immense power, and a willing soul. Ferrin had the shard, and the priests would be there soon enough.

All he needed now was a willing soul. Vius was willing, he knew. Vius would leap off the courtyard and throw himself upon the razor sharp rocks below if Ferrin ordered it. Yet he didn't know if he should sacrifice his remaining apprentice.

Ferrin reached up and ran his finger along the runes etched into the stone. They were smooth and almost seemed to glow under his touch. The life of his body was almost at an end.

He was so close.

Chapter 22

Kira slammed the book shut in frustration. She had read the book from beginning to end three times and had yet to find anything that could help her. She cursed silently and stood up, rubbing her eyes with balled fists. She stared around the room and locked her eyes on the zombie. Who was powerful enough to take over her creation? She wasn't sure. She walked into her bedroom and thought she heard something scrabbling against her wall.

She grabbed her cloak from the dresser and wrapped it around her shoulders. Lifting her hands up before her face, she cast an illusion of a man's appearance over her own. Glancing into a mirror to check that the illusion was flawless, she nodded to herself in satisfaction. She went back into the main room and grabbed her dagger off the table. Placing her leg on a chair, she slid the blade into the sheath she had sewed into her boot. Then she opened the front door and stepped out onto the street.

It was night already. She was surprised at how long she had spent sifting through the book. The sky was clear and the moon was barely a sliver in the blackness. The few lamps that illuminated the street had been lit, but they didn't provide much light. She briefly wondered if that was why all the shady types liked this area of town. She walked the cobblestone path, breathing in the cool night air.

She had been taking walks late in the evening each night for the past week in the hopes of clearing her mind. This night, like the others, would prove to be futile, she knew. She couldn't clear her mind no matter how she tried. Several passages in the book had led her to believe there might be a way to save her child, but she could find nothing definitive.

Subconsciously her hand went to her stomach and she rubbed it gently. She would die before she let her child go to that demon. She walked along the street, passing several run-down homes that lay dark and silent. She could hear the sound of stray cats fighting in an alley close by. Muffled music and the sound of drunken people echoed a few buildings down. Listening to the sounds of the night, she noticed another noise as well.

It was almost imperceptible, but Kira had walked these streets long enough to pick up on things that might seem ordinary to others. She hadn't stayed alive by her magic alone. She began to step cautiously, not sure of where the sound had come from. After a few minutes, she realized she was being followed.

Whoever it was did well to conceal themselves, but she could hear the soft pitter-patter of their footsteps. *If they won't reveal themselves, I'll make them,* she thought.

Kira turned down an alley. Ducking behind a wooden crate, she pushed herself up against the wall, using the natural shadows to hide herself. The footsteps quickened. She reached down and unsheathed the dagger hidden in her boot. Clutching the hilt tightly, she waited. The footsteps stopped and for a moment she thought she lost her follower.

She held her breath and listened intently. Moving as slowly and quietly as she could, she placed her feet in a stance that would allow her to rush whoever walked past the crate. The footsteps resumed, slower this time. She held the pose so long her legs started to burn. She could feel her palm getting sweaty as well. *Hurry up!*

An involuntary tremor began in her right leg. She tried to adjust her position to alleviate the strain on her muscles, to no avail. Suddenly a figure stepped past the crate. Kira drew her dagger back and launched herself forward.

A scream echoed through the alley and Kira pushed the person's head down onto the ground, using her knee to pin the figure down. Kira thought her stalker seemed small, too small. It might not even be a person. Fear fluttered within her stomach as she considered what kind of creature it could be.

The thing struggled against her, flailing wildly. Kira looked out into the street to make sure the scream hadn't attracted any attention. She didn't see anyone. The scream sounded human, but she knew of many creatures that could imitate a human's voice. Gritting her teeth, she lifted the dagger above her head and drove it down with all her might.

Blood spurted over her hand and onto her leg as the blade cut through the back of the creature's neck. She jerked the blade free and stabbed again, severing the spine. The flailing abruptly ended.

Breathing heavily, she fell backward off the thing and wiped the dagger off on her cloak before re-sheathing it. She sat there for a moment to calm her racing heart, then stood up and tried to inspect the body. The darkness of the alley made it too hard to see, so she grabbed the thing's feet, which she noticed had shoes on, and pulled it out into the light of the street.

Kira gasped in horror and felt her stomach wrench. She turned her head and vomited. She spit several times to get the nasty bile out of her mouth and hesitantly looked back at the body.

It was Claire.

Chapter 23

Morell stood on the balcony of his room that afforded him a view overlooking the city. Ravendale was vulnerable now. As the priest considered that thought, he laughed aloud. The city had always been vulnerable, the people just didn't know it.

The Church had become a place to gain wealth and power. That was one of the many reasons Morell had entered the priesthood in the first place. And he had gained much of both. Yet now he found himself bound like a slave to the will of the foul wizard Ferrin. The shard, Morell had come to realize, had not saved him from dying without a price. Part of his soul now resided in the stone.

It wouldn't be such a bad thing if he himself had control of the shard. Unfortunately, that fool Broderick had lost it to Ferrin.

In the distance he could see the short wall that surrounded the city. It wasn't much protection, but it was enough to give the people a peace of mind. Once the failing of the shield had become public knowledge, people had begun to panic.

"Like little scared sheep," the priest said to himself. He had yet to hear any word from Kira. While Ferrin possessed the shard, Morell believed that if anyone could take it back, it would be Broderick. The woodsman had found it after all. Until Ferrin lost control of it, Morell and the others were bound by the power of the shard to obey the wizard.

And now Ferrin had ordered him to send his best priests to the ruins in the Starforge Mountains. He had considered replacing some of the priests with assassins. They could kill the wizard and bring him the shard. He finally decided that would not be the best course of action. Ferrin might suspect betrayal, and Morell wasn't sure if the wizard could read his thoughts through the shard or not.

Reluctantly he had sent just the priests. He didn't know why Ferrin needed them, but he speculated it wasn't for anything good. A knock sounded on the door behind him.

"What is it?" he demanded.

He heard the door open. "The priests have departed, as you asked." It was Justus. Morell turned to face him. The younger priest had been acting odd ever since the shield had fallen.

"Good." Justus bowed and started to leave but Morell told him to stay. "Have you ever seen the city from this view?" he asked Justus.

"I have not," Justus answered.

"Come and look upon my city," Morell said, motioning him to come onto the balcony. Justus hesitated for a moment, then obeyed. They stood staring in silence. "It's beautiful," Justus said finally. Morell smirked. The man was such a soft-hearted fool.

"You remember the day the shield fell?" Morell asked.

"How could I forget?" Justus returned. "You almost died and we were attacked by goblins."

"I did die," Morell replied, chuckling. "An interesting experience, to be sure. Have you ever come close to death?"

Justus stiffened at the question. "No … never."

Morell stared hard at Justus, but the younger priest evaded his gaze. "The man Broderick, you remember him as well?"

Justus nodded slowly. "I do. He saved your life. He is a hero among some of the priests."

Morell snorted in derision. "Hardly. He didn't do anything of his own power. Tell me, did you release him?"

Justus' face reddened and he met Morell's steel gaze with his own. "Why would I betray the Church?" he asked defiantly.

"I didn't ask if you betrayed the Church. I'm asking if you betrayed *me*. Before you try to lie, remember that you are held accountable to the oaths you made when you joined the priesthood."

"What of yourself?" Justus demanded angrily. "I have heard the rumors spoken in secret. You are a murderer and a coward. What of *your* vows? Do they mean nothing to you?" Realizing what he said, he turned his eyes back out toward and city and lowered his head. "Forgive me," he murmured.

Morell casually stepped behind Justus. "I had my fingers crossed when I made my vows," he whispered. Before Justus could turn around, Morell grabbed the priest and pushed him over railing. Justus freefell fifty feet and smashed hard onto the street below. Morell looked down and saw a crowd beginning to gather around the body.

He smiled. *That made me feel better,* he thought.

A searing pain suddenly shot through his neck. He grabbed at his neck desperately and cried out. It was a pain like nothing he had ever felt before. Falling to his knees, he screamed. And then just as suddenly, the pain was gone. Morell collapsed onto the floor of his balcony and there was only darkness.

Chapter 24

Broderick shrieked as he felt a terrible pain at the base of his neck. He released the reins of his horse and instinctively and protectively grabbed his neck. He lost his balance and tumbled from his horse to the ground, landing painfully on his left shoulder.

The pain lanced through his body with abandon, causing him to suck in his breath and hold it. It was all he could do to try not to move. And then the pain was gone. A strong burning sensation overwhelmed his palm. He lay there on the road, fearful to move at all lest the pain return. He noticed Marc was crouched near him, worry in the soldier's eyes.

"Are you all right?" he asked.

Broderick heaved air into his lungs. "I'm not sure," he managed to get out. Marc held out his hand to offer Broderick help. He hesitated, then accepted the help and got onto his feet. He gingerly touched his neck, but there was no pain.

"What happened?" Marc asked, looking over him to make sure he wasn't wounded. "I'm not sure," Broderick reiterated. "Pain just shot through my neck. It was the worst feeling I think I've ever experienced." A dull throbbing started to pound in Broderick's head. "My head hurts," he said. He began rubbing his temples.

"Should we make camp?" Marc asked him. Broderick shook his head. "No, I'm fine now. Let's continue as planned."

Broderick placed his foot in the stirrups and heaved himself onto his horse. Nae'fir rode up next to him and spoke a soft command to stop his own horse. Broderick looked at him and smiled wanly. "I'm fine," he said before the elf could question him. It was weird seeing a human appearance on the elf.

Before they had set out, Nae'fir had altered his appearance to keep Broderick's guards from realizing that it was elves that lived in the forest. They had also cleverly set up a camp and Broderick used a false story to make them believe they had not even entered the woods, but that they had dreamed seeing figures in the trees.

Nae'fir pointed to Broderick's hand. Looking down, he saw that some blood had seeped from the open wound on his palm. "It's never done that before," he said. The elf looked like he was deep in thought. "I am not sure what it could mean, but I fear we must quicken our pace. If it has something to do with the shard, there is no telling what danger lies ahead for you. Come." Nae'fir took the lead, urging his mount to travel quickly with a spoken command.

"I should have trained my horse like that," Ged remarked. Broderick smiled but didn't say anything. *If they only knew,* he thought. They all followed after the elf, their horses struggling to keep pace. Marc was suspicious of Nae'fir when he first joined them. Broderick had told them he was the person they had traveled so far to find, but Marc had difficulty believing anyone could live in the dead forest. With a bit of storytelling, Broderick eventually convinced Marc that Nae'fir was no threat to them, and that he had traveled there to meet them.

They were headed north-west, taking almost the same route they had when traveling to the forest. Nae'fir had told him that they had to get a fair distance away from the forest in order for Broderick to trace the shard with his connection. He explained the humming sound Broderick had heard was from the magic of the elves that kept the plague at bay.

It also prevented most magic from being used within the forest. Broderick had tried to focus on his bond with the shard the previous night, to no avail. As they continued, Broderick wondered how Kira was doing. He almost wished they could go back to Myrwood, at least so he could see her, but he knew that time was their most valuable commodity. The faster they found the shard, the faster they could break the deal with Skiram.

They rode at a steady pace until dusk, when Marc forced them all to stop and let the horses rest. After they set up camp, they shared a meal of rabbit stew and bread, which Broderick found to be delicious after the less than filling food he ate with the elves.

They sat around the fire for a few hours after eating, the soldier's sharing war stories and relating tales of heros of old. Nae'fir listened intently to them all, nodding at certain points as if he was agreeing with their stories. Broderick stared at the orange flames. Fire seemed to always remind him of that cursed demon now. Occasionally, a loud *pop* would ring out.

"What about you?" Marc asked Nae'fir. "Are you a soldier?"

Nae'fir shook his head. "I am no warrior, but that does not mean I have not seen battle. I even participated in a few, but I did not care for the shedding of blood."

"Tell us a story then," Joel said. "Surely you have something we have never heard. You live farther than any of us have ventured, so perhaps you have a story none of us have heard?"

Nae'fir pressed his fingers together and nodded. "Perhaps. Have you heard the tale of Norran? I did not think so. In the beginning of time, when all things were newly created, Norran was given charge of a chest that contained all the world's wisdom. The Creator had given it to him with the instruction that he should share the wisdom with everyone. Each day Norran looked into the chest and learned new things.

"The chest was full of various beliefs and ways of thinking. Norran grew covetous and refused to share the wisdom with anyone else. He decided to hide the chest of wisdom in the tallest tree he could find. Using vines, he made strong rope and tied it around the chest and tied the chest to the front of his body. He attempted to climb the tree, but struggled because the chest hindered him from climbing.

"Nearby, a child watched in rapt fascination. Then the child laughed and told him, 'If you tie the chest to your back, it will be easier to climb the tree.' Norran took the child's advice and was able to climb to the top of the tree. When he reached the top, he grew angry and thought to himself, *A child has more sense than I, and I hold the chest of wisdom.* So he threw the chest of wisdom out of the tree.

"It smashed upon the ground, and wisdom flew in all directions. As time passed, people found pieces of wisdom and took them home. That is why no single person holds all the world's wisdom, for it is scattered throughout the earth."

No one spoke as Nae'fir finished his story. Broderick imagined the entire story in his mind. The elf seemed to have the ability to sculpt images with his words. "That's an interesting tale," Ged said, breaking the silence. Everyone shared their accord.

"It's time to retire for the night, I think," Marc said, standing up and stretching his legs. "We've got an early start in the morning." No one argued with him. They appointed Joel for the first watch, and everyone else laid down to rest.

Broderick lay on his back staring up at the night sky. Wisps of cloud dotted the sky's canvas, but they couldn't blot out the stars. They shone brightly, and he could see several constellations. He saw the Warrior, holding his sword up and keeping the peace. His mother always pointed that one out when he was younger. Numerous memories of his mother came to mind, and he reminisced of the simpler times in his life.

He also thought of Nae'fir's story and wondered if it were true. It seemed absurd that all of the world's wisdom could be kept in a chest, but he also found the idea that elves were real beings absurd. Yet here was one with him now, traveling to defeat an evil wizard and take back a fallen piece of the sun.

The whole thing sounded like something a crazed drunk would invent. His drifted off to sleep thinking about Kira and their unborn child.

His eyes fluttered open and he saw Nae'fir crouched beside him. The elf motioned for Broderick to follow him. He looked over to where Joel was keeping watch and saw him slumped down on the ground. Rising onto his feet, he followed the elf a fair distance from the camp.

"What is it?" Broderick asked.

"Try to locate the shard," Nae'fir instructed.

"Now? Could it not have waited until morning?"

Nae'fir pursed his lips. "We need to know where it is before we travel any further. And your soldiers can't go with us, so we need to leave them here."

Broderick's face scrunched up. "What? Why wouldn't we take them with us? We might need their protection. *I* might need their protection."

Nae'fir sighed. "Once Ferrin and I engage in battle, I won't have the strength to keep up this illusion. I will not allow the secret of my people's existence to be revealed. If those soldiers see me, they will put things together and realize your story has many flaws in it. They will return to my homeland and I know what will happen."

"How do you know what will happen?"

"I have seen it before."

The words evoked powerful memories into Broderick's consciousness. Trees burning, elves being killed, and humans running around, causing it all. Broderick shook his head and the images left.

"I will keep them from finding your homeland, but I will not go against Ferrin without them. If you cannot agree to this, then you are on your own to get the shard."

They stood in silence gazing at one another. Finally, Nae'fir agreed. Closing his eyes, Broderick focused on the wound in his palm. He felt a slight tingle, similar to the feeling of a limb falling asleep. He wasn't sure how to connect his mind to the shard, so he focused on the tingling. It began to spread from his palm throughout his entire body.

And then the feeling faded, and he felt like he was falling. He opened his eyes and everything was chaos. Swirling lights of all colors burst like explosions before him. He felt so very hot, and yet he was freezing at the same moment. He could see the beginning and the end of all things. Everything swirled around him, and then he saw golden lights that looked like threads floating freely.

Broderick thought them curious things and he drew closer to them. They pulsed rhythmically before his eyes, reminding him of a heartbeat. He started to reach out to one when he felt something behind him. He turned and felt a darkness sweep through, enveloping him. It wasn't like the dark of night. There was something sinister about it. The darkness radiated from a corner, and he floated toward it.

Broderick pushed himself through the darkness and everything flipped upside down. Or perhaps it was right side up. He became so disoriented, he wasn't sure about anything. And then a hazy image came into focus. Gray pillars. Mountains. And Vius tracing something on a stone floor. Before he could begin to feel confusion, he felt his mind being assaulted by another.

Memories flashed before him. They didn't make any sense. And then he saw himself. He was looking at himself, only how was that possible? He looked down and saw he was wearing black robes. His eyes widened as he realized he wasn't himself, but he was Ferrin. He was *in* Ferrin.

Suddenly he felt as though he were being pulled backwards. The exploding lights and the golden threads blurred past him and he found himself standing in front of Nae'fir. He looked around, confused.

"What did you see?" Nae'fir questioned.

"Things I didn't understand," Broderick answered, still reeling from the experience. "I saw ruins of an old building. And mountains. Ferrin's apprentice was there, drawing something. I don't know what it was. I'm not sure … but I think I was in his body."

"Ferrin's body?"

"Yes," Broderick answered. His knees buckled and gave out on him. He slumped down onto the ground with a groan.

"Did you see anything else?"

Broderick nodded. "Yes. I saw a glimpse into his mind, I think. There were many things, most of them I couldn't understand. But there was one thing I saw clearly. He is going to break open the shard."

Chapter 25

Over the next few days, they drove their horses beyond exhaustion. Broderick's own mount ended up dying, which caused them to lose precious time. He rode with Marc on his horse until they reached a small town where they could buy another.

They didn't spend much time resting, choosing instead to push themselves as hard as their horses. Marc and the others didn't say a word in protest, but Broderick knew they were not happy with their suicidal pace. He wished he could share the reason for their haste with them, but Nae'fir had sworn him to keep silent.

They had almost passed through the Great Plains, and after that, they would reach the mountains where, according to Nae'fir, they would find Ferrin. They had stopped to eat one night, and Broderick questioned the elf in private about the place he had seen through Ferrin's eyes.

"What is it?"

Nae'fir finished chewing some berries he had found at their last campsite. "It is a place older than memory," he said. He took a sip from a flask he had brought with him filled with *shekhar*. "Even the oldest among my people do not know its origins. It was first brought to our attention before my kind closed our boundaries. One of my fellow spell weavers had fallen in love with a human woman.

"She was a pilgrim and had traveled across the land, searching out forgotten holy sites. She took him there and showed him the wonders of the place. When he returned, he shared what he had seen with myself and the king.

"With a few others, we traveled to the ruins and investigated the area." Nae'fir looked into the sky, staring at the stars in silence for a moment. "What we found was as intriguing as it was disturbing."

Broderick scratched his chin and waited for the elf to continue talking. When he didn't, Broderick spoke up. "What did you find?"

"Spells. Hundreds of spells, etched into the walls of a cave. That was the intriguing part. The disturbing aspect was the design of the cave. It was a natural cave, formed over the course of time. Yet the inside had been changed. There was something strange about the floor, but we were unable to determine what it was exactly, or its purpose.

"For several years I searched through everything in my personal library, as well as the King's. I found nothing useful, but I continued to search no matter. The writing was very close to elvish, but none of my people have ever lived outside of the forest. I don't know who could have designed that place, but I suspect they might have been an elf."

"So what is the purpose of the place?" Broderick asked.

"I have never been able to discern that. I was able to decipher a portion of one of the spells on the wall. It referenced holy blood. Blood magic is ancient, and most wizards today don't even know of its existence."

"Most? Does Ferrin know about it?"

Nae'fir frowned. "Unfortunately, I believe he may. That is why we must hurry and reach the mountains. If Ferrin plans to break open the shard, nothing good can come from it."

Broderick didn't argue with that. They walked back to camp and after laying back down, Nae'fir released the spell on Joel. The young soldier shook himself awake, glanced around, and resumed his post as if nothing had happened. Broderick smiled and tried to go to sleep.

Dawn came too quickly for his liking, but he knew that they had to get moving. Rousing himself from his bedroll, he found the soldiers already up and eating breakfast. He didn't see Nae'fir anywhere. Broderick walked over to the fire and poured himself the last of what was in the pot.

He didn't bother asking what it was and devoured it quickly. He was about to ask Marc where Nae'fir was when the elf rode up on his horse. "I see tracks," he said, pointing northward. "A large group on foot, it seems. They're headed the same direction as us." The tone of his voice hinted to Broderick that this was more bad news.

"Let's go," Broderick said. They broke down their camp in a matter of minutes. Broderick always marveled at the efficiency and quickness with which the soldiers did everything. They rode out shortly after that, following the trail of tracks.

After almost an hour, they came upon the group that had made the tracks. They were a fair distance away, but Broderick recognized the unmistakable white robes of priests immediately. "Priests," he stated, nodding in the direction of the travelers. "A bunch of them." Looking to Nae'fir, he saw the elf seemed troubled, more so than before.

He pulled his horse next to Nae'fir's and in a low voice asked, "What is it?"

"I'm not sure. A feeling, mostly. Yet I think that these priests are not here by coincidence, considering the direction of their course, and who waits there." Broderick nodded. He had come to the same conclusion.

"What should we do?" he asked Nae'fir.

"I have an idea," the elf answered, "though it may be tricky. Let you and I overtake them, and leave the others here. Then …" as Nae'fir finished explaining his plan, Broderick shared it with Marc. The soldier was hesitant, but agreed to do as he was instructed.

Broderick and Nae'fir rode forth and met up with the priests after a few minutes. "Good men," Broderick greeted them as they approached. The group of holy men slowed their pace but they did not stop. "I hate to trouble you gentlemen, but we have just been struck with disaster. My comrades are stuck, and we could use some assistance. Would you be so kind?" He slowed his horse to keep step beside the lead priests.

"We would love to help," one of them said, "but we are on a holy pilgrimage to the mountains. If we were not pressed for time, we would most assuredly help you. I beg your apology."

Broderick thought it might prove difficult to get them to agree, and he had prepared an argument in advance. "We were just riding along, and a giant sinkhole opened up and swallowed my comrades. All five of them went right down into the ground. I don't need all of you to help, just a few strong men to help us lift them out with some rope. If you can be so kind as to spare them long enough to help, we can ride them back to meet you. No time lost, really. What do you say?"

The priest continued walking for a moment and then nodded his acceptance. "That should be fine." Without stopping, he identified five men from the group and told them to follow Broderick. "I appreciate it," Broderick said as he turned his horse around. The priest nodded.

Broderick and Nae'fir led the priests back to where Marc and the others were waiting. As they led them into a patch of tall grass, the soldiers leapt out and attacked the priests. None of them used weapons, as they did not want to kill them. They easily overpowered them and knocked them unconscious.

"I hope you have a good reason for this," Ged remarked to Broderick. "I don't see how assaulting priests is going to help me after I die."

"It can't be helped," Broderick answered. "Just trust me. It's for the best."

Ged grunted in response.

They bound the priests to each other with rope and took their robes from them, leaving them huddled together in the grass with only their loincloths. Marc and the other soldiers donned the robes and remounted their horses.

"We've taken too long. Let us hurry," Nae'fir said. They thundered back to the north, pausing to leave the 'priests' with their group. "Thanks again!"

Broderick yelled to them as he and Nae'fir continued on. They tied the soldiers' horses to their own to keep from having to leave them behind.

"We must reach the mountains before they do," Nae'fir said.

"Do you think Ferrin will know?" Broderick asked, worried for Marc and the others.

"We can only hope that he does not."

They continued riding in silence much of the day, pausing only once to eat and give the horses a brief respite. By the time the sun set, they had reached the base of the Starforge Mountains.

"We are making camp?" Broderick asked as he dismounted, rubbing his sore legs.

"No," Nae'fir answered. "We must leave the horses here and continue on foot through the night. We do not have time to rest."

Broderick groaned. "We don't have time to rest at all?"

Nae'fir shook his head. "No. Stand on that rock," he pointed. Out of curiosity, Broderick obeyed. "What do you see?" the elf asked him.

"Nothing," Broderick answered.

"Look to the horizon," Nae'fir instructed.

Broderick turned his gaze to the way they had come. At first he didn't see anything. Then he noticed movement. He squinted to try and see better, but it was no use. "What is it?" he said, still squinting.

"The priests."

"What? How have they traveled so fast?"

Nae'fir dismounted his own horse and spoke a few whispered words to the creature. It turned and trotted off to the east. "My assumption would be that they are aided by magic. There was something about the one we spoke to that seemed out of the ordinary. I believe he was carrying a charm of some sort. It seems Ferrin understands the importance of time as we do."

"Then let us waste no more of it."

They began their ascent of the mountain immediately and Broderick struggled with every step. The terrain of the mountain was rocky and loose. He found himself ankle deep in the dirt, his legs burning with the tremendous effort it took to free his feet and continue. Nae'fir seemed to have no difficulty at all, stepping lightly and easily.

Broderick was heaving, his breath coming in short, ragged gasps. Every step was excruciating. He desperately wanted to stop and take a break, but he feared if he stopped he wouldn't be able to continue. Sweat drenched his body, making his clothes cling to his flesh uncomfortably.

His foot yanked free of his boot and he stabbed the bottom of his foot on an uneven rock. He cursed in his mind but forced his body to continue. His other foot came free of his boot and he continued barefoot. The soil clung to his sweat laden skin. He forced his mind to focus on lifting his foot and stomping it down.

It became a litany. Up, down. Up, down. Up, down. He kept his eyes focused of Nae'fir's back and repeated the citation over and over. Hours passed without his notice. His muscles were so sore and tired that he became numb to it.

At some point he became aware of a faint light in the sky. He almost ran into Nae'fir before he realized the elf had stopped. "What is it?" Broderick croaked, his voice breaking. He was extremely thirsty. His legs shook violently and he collapsed onto his backside.

"I'm surprised you haven't fainted yet," the elf said calmly, as if he had expended no effort. Nae'fir handed Broderick a wooden flask. He took a drink of the elvish liquid. A feeling like fire swept through his body, invigorating him. He handed the flask back to the elf and leaned against a rock.

"We are almost to the ruins. Take your rest now, for we must be ready and focused if we intend to face one such as Ferrin."

Chapter 26

Broderick crouched beside a crumbling pillar of gray marble. He risked a glance into the courtyard of the ruins and ducked back behind the column. The priests stood in a circle, hands clasped together. He saw another man dressed similar to the priests standing to the side.

He looked to where Nae'fir said he would be but he didn't see the elf. He wondered what Marc and the other soldiers were thinking then. He couldn't tell which of the men in the courtyard they were, but he knew they were down there. All twenty were accounted for. He didn't see Ferrin. If he had to guess, he assumed the other man was Vius, the foul wizard's apprentice.

Broderick remembered his encounter with that one well. He rubbed his jaw subconsciously just thinking about the painful blow he had sustained at the man's hands. He noticed the tingling in his palm had returned as well. He hoped Nae'fir knew what he was doing. There wouldn't be much to do except die if they failed, Ferrin would see to that.

He looked to the sky when he heard a rumble in the distance. Dark clouds were coming their way. He could make out the flashing of lightning in their black depths, illuminating the darkness of the clouds here and there.

A loud *thud* turned his attention back to the courtyard. One of the priests lay dead, his blood pooling onto the floor. For some unknown reason, the other priests didn't move. He watched Vius walk to the next in line. The man held a dagger to the priest's neck and slit the flesh. He dropped to the floor also, blood spilling everywhere. *Why were they just standing there?*

Concern gripped him as he considered the fact that Vius could be killing the soldiers disguised as priests. He couldn't just sit there and wait for Nae'fir to offer a signal. He looked to his palm. Focusing on the showing bone, he thrust his mind into the connection with the shard. He was assailed by the bright lights he had seen before.

They flashed and pulsed, blinding him temporarily. He blinked until his vision cleared. He saw the golden threads floating through the shard. He was tempted to touch them, but he reminded himself he didn't have time. He wasn't sure how to channel the power to obey his will, so he tried speaking it aloud.

Nothing happened.

He found the blackness and he hovered near it. If he did as he did before, he might not get away from Ferrin's mind unscathed. And it was entirely possible that the wizard would be alerted to his presence. He considered his dilemma.

Perhaps Ferrin was using the shard to keep the priests bound in one spot? Broderick closed his eyes and tried to look beyond the shard. He could feel something in the air, some sort of barrier around the priests. He tried to shift it, but it felt heavy and immovable. He changed tactics, concentrating on a portion of the barrier instead of the whole thing.

He tried to determine which of the men was Marc. He picked one and hoped it was him. Concentrating on the barrier around the man, he tried move it. At first it seemed like it was futile. But he kept pushing, forcing his mind to find a weakness.

And then he felt it budge. It wasn't much, but it was enough to give him the hope that he could free the barrier from holding the man. With a groan of pain, he felt the barrier fall away from the man. And just before he felt his mind surge back into his body, he watched Vius slit another priest's throat.

Broderick snapped his eyes open. He thought it had only taken him a few minutes to displace the barrier, but the storm was almost above him now. He looked down into the courtyard and saw Vius poised to kill another man. He growled in frustration and looked to where Nae'fir was supposed to be. He still didn't see the elf. A flash of lightning lit up the darkened sky. A loud clap of thunder followed soon after. The wind began blowing harshly.

Where are you, elf?

And then he saw Nae'fir reveal himself from his hiding spot. He gave the signal. Broderick began to move slowly and quietly toward the center of the courtyard. Vius stole the life from two more of the priests. Bile rose up Broderick's throat, and he had to swallow quickly to keep from vomiting. His throat burned like fire, but he ignored the pain. He had to hurry.

He slipped on a loose rock and fell on his face. He stayed where he was, hoping no one heard the noise. After a few seconds, he decided it was safe and rose back to his feet. He peered around the column in front of him. Vius was gone. Cursing his luck, he tried to determine where the wizard was without showing himself.

One of the priests, the one he removed the barrier from, removed himself from the circle and threw his robes off. It was Ged. Broderick had hoped to free Marc, but Ged was certainly better than not freeing anyone. The tall soldier brandished his claymore and hid himself in the shadows.

Still not seeing Vius, Broderick decided to move closer. A jarring force slammed into the side of his head and he went sprawling onto the ground again. He saw through blurred vision that Vius was standing over him.

"Fool! Did you think you could come here unnoticed?"

Broderick clenched his eyes shut as a wave of pain overwhelmed him. He felt something heavy against his chest and realized that Vius had him pinned to the ground with his foot. "I don't know what you are planning, but it's not going to happen," Broderick spat. Vius leaned down and pressed the dagger he had used to kill the priests to his neck. The look in the man's eyes was all Broderick needed to know that he was about to die.

And then a flurry of motion in his peripheral caught his attention. Ged tackled Vius, the two of them tumbling to the ground. Broderick forced himself onto his feet and ran toward the others priests. He had to free them somehow.

"Wake up! Quickly, get out of here!" he shouted, trying to get their attention. None of them responded or moved. He started pulling their hoods back, looking for Marc. Thunder rumbled overheard, causing the loose rocks to clatter.

Broderick felt a hand on his shoulder and turned. "Ged," he said, but froze in terror as he looked upon Vius. The wizard had a horrible gash across his stomach. He punched Broderick in the mouth, making him stumble backward from the force.

"Where are the other priests?" Vius demanded angrily. Broderick used the back of his hand to wipe the blood from his mouth. The wizard stalked toward him dangerously.

A ball of white light slammed into Vius, flinging him across the courtyard. Broderick turned to see Nae'fir, the rough wind ripping at his robes. "I thought you'd never come," he said to the elf.

Nae'fir ignored him and walked toward the end of the ruins, disappearing into the cave. Broderick was unsure of what to do. He went back to the priests and found Marc. The soldier seemed to be coherent, but he couldn't speak. His eyes moved around furiously.

"I'm trying to free you," Broderick told him. Marc's eyes widened in fear and Broderick turned to see Vius making his way toward him. The fake priestly garments were burned to a crisp and the skin that was visible was blackened.

Why won't he die?

Vius reached out to grab him, but Broderick ducked under his arm. He circled around the wizard and grabbed Vius's dagger off the ground. Lunging after the wizard, he tried to stab him in the chest. Vius sidestepped, missing the worst, but Broderick grazed his shoulder with the blade.

Vius growled in a mixture of anger and pain. Broderick swung the dagger back and forth, trying to hit the man. Vius stepped forward and under the swinging blade, grabbing Broderick's arm and twisting his wrist. Pain lanced through Broderick's arm and he involuntarily loosened his grip on the dagger.

The blade clanged harmlessly to the ground. Vius kicked Broderick in the knee. His legs were already weakened from the climb up the mountain and he crumbled to the ground, gasping in pain. Vius picked the dagger up and grabbed Broderick's hair, forcing his head back.

The tingling in Broderick's palm flared up again, and a desperate idea roared through his mind. He grabbed onto Vius's leg and imagined flames bursting from his hand. Everything seemed like it was moving in slow motion. Vius's dagger was coming at his exposed neck. The wind was blowing. Lightning crackled across the sky. Thunder shook the ground beneath them.

Broderick blinked. The dagger seemed to take forever to reach him. And then Vius's arm stopped mid-swing. His arm had hit an invisible barrier and flung the blade from his hand. And then bright orange and yellow flames poured out of his hand and onto Vius's robes, engulfing the man in a raging inferno. He scrambled back away from the burning wizard. The man's agonized screams tore at his heart.

For a moment, he felt bad for Vius. To die by being burned alive, feeling your skin shrivel off your muscles. Vius fell onto the ground, flailing and thrashing. Broderick averted his eyes and saw Ged staggering across the courtyard, covered in blood. His or Vius's, he wasn't sure.

And then it began to rain. Huge drops of water fell from the storm clouds, splattering everything. It came down hard, pouring fiercely and drenching everything. Broderick crawled over to the ring of priests and noticed the water mixing with the blood on the ground.

A torrent of black flames came rushing from out of the cave, and Broderick dropped down to the ground to keep from being burned. He heard a whirring sound and then suddenly Ferrin and Nae'fir were standing in the courtyard.

They were flinging spells of all types at one another. Black flames, fiery darts, gleaming balls of light. It was happening so fast, Broderick barely saw their lips moving. It seemed like they took turns rushing the other, magic flaring to life and then sizzling out. It was an epic battle that kept Broderick mesmerized. He barely noticed the barrier had lifted and the priests were scrambling to get out of the place.

Ferrin slammed the end of his staff onto the ground. The stone tiles around Nae'fir cracked and shifted down, threatening to sink the elf into the ground. The elf leapt into the air and seemed to hover there while a bluish haze of energy flared from his palm and struck Ferrin in the chest. The wizard flew ten feet and crashed into a pillar, the old marble crumbling under the force.

Nae'fir wasted no time and dropped back to the ground, running to where Ferrin had fallen. A massive fireball struck the elf full force.

Broderick heard a whisper in his ear. *Get the shard and flee! It's in the cave!*

He wasn't sure, but he thought it was the voice of Nae'fir. He watched the two fling magic at each other for a moment more, then hurried into the cave. Flowing script covered every inch of the walls. The darkness was lightened somewhat by the shard, which hung suspended over a strange rune on the floor.

Broderick didn't have time to ponder what Ferrin was attempting to do. He grabbed the shard and stuffed it into a pouch on his belt. He saw Marc enter the cave.

"What in the name of Raven is happening?"

"I'll explain later. We've got to get out of here! Get the others and let's go." They ran back into the courtyard and Marc yelled for the others to follow them.

Ferrin had a whip made of green light and was trying to strike Nae'fir. The elf dashed to the left and right, easily avoiding the wizard's magical weapon. Nae'fir placed his hands together, side by side, and faced his palms towards Ferrin. He spoke one word, "*Qerach!*"

Frost began to collect around Ferrin's legs, holding him in place and slowly spreading up his body. Nae'fir turned to Broderick. "Here," he threw something at him, which Broderick barely caught. He held it up. It was some sort of crystal. "Use it against the demon! Now go, before—"

Ferrin used his staff to smash through the ice, then swung the staff horizontally, connecting a solid blow to the side of Nae'fir's head.

Broderick didn't want to leave the elf, but he didn't have any choice. There was nothing he could do to help. As he turned to flee, a bolt of jagged lightning dropped from the sky and struck the dueling wizards. The flash blinded Broderick. A few seconds later, an invisible force sent him flying backwards, slamming roughly into one of the pillars.

He lay there blinded for what seemed like an eternity. Slowly the light faded from his eyes and he was able to make out his surroundings. He sat up and rubbed the back of his head. A pounding headache assaulted him. And his hand was covered in blood. Tears stung his eyes at the pain and he dared not move for fear he had broken something.

Marc came into view, staggering towards him.

His mouth was moving, but Broderick couldn't hear anything. It was then he noticed his ears were ringing. It was an odd sensation not being able to hear. He stared dumbly at the soldier and could only shake his head. Marc knelt down in front of him, tears streaming down his face. He kept talking. Broderick tried futilely to read his lips, but it didn't do any good. He couldn't focus long enough.

Marc eventually gave up. After half of an hour, Broderick noticed he was starting to hear again. The rumbling of thunder first. And then he heard the rain as it struck the ground. He stood up, his legs unsteady beneath him. He waited until he had his balance before trying to walk.

And then he saw the reason for Marc's tears. Joel, the young soldier, lay face down. He was dead. A gaping wound in his head gave Broderick an idea as to how he had died. Broderick himself could have just as easily met the same fate. He knelt down and laid his hand on Joel's body. Nothing happened. He didn't understand why the shard didn't bring him back.

Rising back to his feet, he looked around. Ferrin and Nae'fir were nowhere to be seen. The gray stones where they had been standing when the lightning struck were charred and melted. The forces of nature were a scary thing.

Marc gathered the others, but no one spoke. A heaviness pervaded the air. The storm had begun to subside, but the damage was already done. They began their descent down the mountain, the effort much less than it took to climb it.

As they went, they came across several dead priests who had apparently fallen down the jagged terrain in their flight.

When they reached the base of the mountain an hour later, the sun was shining. The clouds had rolled off to the east. Broderick was the first to notice that the horses were gone. They had probably fled when the storm came.

They all stood there, staring in different directions. Finally, Broderick sighed and brushed some dirt off his shirt.

"It's going to be a long walk home," he said.

"That it is," Ged muttered. "That it is."

ABOUT THE AUTHOR

Hey there!

I write fantasy and space opera, and you can find all my books in many different ebook stores. You can check out my website for more information about my books, my next projects, and events I'll be attending.

If you enjoyed this book, I'd love your feedback in the form of a review on Amazon or Goodreads.

Thanks for reading!

-Richard

Website: www.richardfierce.com

Facebook: www.facebook.com/dragonfirepress

TikTok: www.tiktok.com/TTPdSrPTBx